Bigotry

Bigotry

Look for these and other books in the Lucent Overview Series:

Abortion
Acid Rain
Adoption
Advertising
Alcoholism
Animal Rights
Artificial Organs
The Beginning of Writing
The Brain
Cancer
Censorship
Child Abuse
Children's Rights
Cities
The Collapse of the Soviet Union
Cults
Dealing with Death
Death Penalty
Democracy
Drug Abuse
Drugs and Sports
Drug Trafficking
Eating Disorders
Elections
Endangered Species
The End of Apartheid in South Africa
Energy Alternatives
Espionage
Ethnic Violence
Euthanasia
Extraterrestrial Life
Family Violence
Gangs
Garbage
Gay Rights
Genetic Engineering
The Greenhouse Effect
Gun Control
Hate Groups
Hazardous Waste
The Holocaust

Homeless Children
Homelessness
Illegal Immigration
Illiteracy
Immigration
Juvenile Crime
Memory
Mental Illness
Militias
Money
Ocean Pollution
Oil Spills
The Olympic Games
Organ Transplants
Ozone
The Palestinian-Israeli Accord
Pesticides
Police Brutality
Population
Poverty
Prisons
Rainforests
The Rebuilding of Bosnia
Recycling
The Reunification of Germany
Schools
Smoking
Space Exploration
Special Effects in the Movies
Sports in America
Suicide
The UFO Challenge
The United Nations
The U.S. Congress
The U.S. Presidency
Vanishing Wetlands
Vietnam
Women's Rights
World Hunger
Zoos

Bigotry

by Debbie Levy

Lucent
Books

Library of Congress Cataloging-in-Publication Data

Levy, Debbie.
 Bigotry / by Debbie Levy.
    p. cm. — (Lucent overview series)
Includes bibliographical references (p.) and index.
Summary: Presents a historical view of causes and effects of stereotypes,
hate groups, hate crimes, and the legal and other methods used to combat
them, with emphasis on recent incidents in the United States.
 ISBN 1-56006-500-1
 1. Toleration—Juvenile literature. 2. Toleration—United States—
Juvenile literature. [1. Toleration. 2. Prejudices. 3. Discrimination.
4. Hate crimes. 5. Hate Groups.] I. Title. II. Series.
 HM1271 .L48 2002
 179'.9—dc21
                                                    2001003017

Copyright © 2002 by Lucent Books, Inc.
P.O. Box 289011, San Diego, CA 92198-9011
Printed in the U.S.A.

Contents

Introduction

JOHN ROCKER SEEMED to be going for some sort of record—how many bigoted remarks one person could make in a single magazine interview. "The biggest thing I don't like about New York," he told the reporter, "are the foreigners. I'm not a very big fan of foreigners. You can walk an entire block in Times Square and not hear anybody speaking English. Asians and Koreans and Vietnamese and Indians and Russians and Spanish people and everything up there. How . . . did they get in this country?"[1]

Rocker, a relief pitcher for the Atlanta Braves, was not finished. He wanted to explain why he would never play baseball for a New York team. "Imagine having to take the . . . train to the ballpark," he said, "looking like you're [riding through] Beirut next to some kid with purple hair next to some queer with AIDS right next to some dude who just got out of jail for the fourth time right next to some 20-year-old mom with four kids." As if to clinch the record, Rocker, who is white, also referred to an African American teammate as "a fat monkey."[2]

When the interview with John Rocker was published in the December 1999 issue of *Sports Illustrated*, millions of readers were taken aback. Rocker's bigoted comments became the talk of radio call-in shows and the stuff of newspaper columns.

American as apple pie

Many people were deeply offended by John Rocker's remarks. But there is no question that many other Americans share Rocker's views, or at least identify with some of them. In some ways, bigotry is as American as apple pie—and baseball.

Bigotry is prejudice against and intolerance of people who are different. Bigoted people often prejudge others who belong to racial, religious, ethnic, or national groups that are different from their group. Bigotry can also extend to people who are different by virtue of their sexual orientation, disability, or age. Prejudice generally causes a bigoted person to judge others negatively based on traits such as skin color, religion, or nationality. Bigots also discriminate against people who are different—meaning that they treat those people less favorably simply because they can be categorized, for example, as black, or Jewish, or gay.

Many people were outraged by Atlanta Braves pitcher John Rocker's bigoted comments that were quoted in a Sports Illustrated *article.*

Some people, like John Rocker, voice bigoted ideas. These ideas may be the private comments of a parent to a child about the supposed inferiority of "those people"—whether "those people" are black, Jewish, Latino, or otherwise. Or they may be the very public rantings of a performer such as the rapper Eminem. Eminem, whose real name is Marshall Mathers, has won fame, fortune, and criticism, in part based on his brutal lyrics that attack homosexuals and women. The words to one of Eminem's songs that gained popularity in 2000 include the following:

Successful rapper Eminem has been criticized for his inflammatory lyrics against women and homosexuals.

My words are like a dagger with a jagged edge
That'll stab you in the head whether you're a fag or lez. . . .
Hate fags?
The answer's "yes."[3]

The album containing this song, and another with similar lyrics, sold millions of copies in 2000, second only to the recordings of the popular group 'N Sync.

"Prejudice is . . . contagious"

Bigotry is not limited to whispered comments and shouted rap lyrics. It is also the inspiration behind actions that have tangible effects on their targets. Shopkeepers and restaurant employees sometimes treat African American customers worse than they treat white customers. Employers sometimes discriminate against gay workers. Members of social clubs sometimes bar Jewish people from joining. Children sometimes exclude Asian American children from neighborhood games. The list could go on and on. Sometimes the actions inspired by bigoted thinking are more extreme, such as the vandalism of Jewish synagogues or African American churches or assaults on people who appear to be of Hispanic heritage, or gay, or Native American.

John Rocker later apologized for his bigoted remarks and said he was not a racist. Rapper Eminem has suggested that his bigoted lyrics may not represent his true feelings. In an interview with *Rolling Stone* magazine, he said, "The kids listening to my music get the joke. They can tell when I'm serious and when I'm not."[4]

Regardless of whether Eminem is serious or joking, and whether John Rocker is apologetic or a racist, the controversies they created highlight the continuing struggle over bigotry in the United States. Bigotry affects nearly every aspect of life, from work to play to housing to shopping. The problem of bigotry is not merely that it is not "nice" to judge others based on characteristics such as skin color or religion. The problem is that those judgments harm the people being judged. Bigotry excludes people from opportunities—in school, work, and elsewhere—because of factors, such as skin color, that are irrelevant to the opportunity being denied.

While rap lyrics and offhanded comments by a professional athlete may not be the central problem of bigotry, they do suggest just how deeply planted bigoted attitudes are in American society. As a young student recently told the authors of a book about bigotry among children, "Sometimes when the kids single out a person and they start making fun of him, at first I object and I don't take part in it. But then, after a while, I start thinking like them and I laugh, too. Prejudice is sort of contagious."[5]

Prejudice is contagious. How seriously it infects American society and whether there are antidotes for it are pressing issues for the twenty-first century.

1

The Many Faces of Bigotry

Jews are cunning businesspeople.
Italians are emotional.
Asians are smart in math but bad at sports.
Blacks are good athletes but poor students.
White men can't jump.

THESE ARE ALL common stereotypes about various ethnic and racial groups. Although they are not uniformly negative—Asians are smart in math, and blacks are good athletes—such stereotypes are the seeds from which bigotry grows. A stereotype is a generalization about a group of people that ignores actual differences among the members of that group. Stereotypes characterize the group and all its members without the benefit of actual knowledge or understanding of the individual members of the group.

Everyone uses stereotypes. Indeed, stereotypes seem to be useful, and even necessary, tools that help human beings make sense of the world around them. After all, a stereotype is a category, and putting people, places, and things in categories is the way the human intellect deals with vast amounts of information. A hiker who sees a bear in the woods does not need to interact with that particular bear to understand the potential danger. He or she categorizes the bear as an animal that poses a danger and quickly takes appropriate action to avoid the danger.

But bigotry takes categories a step beyond their usefulness. According to Dr. John Bargh of New York University, "Stereotypes are categories that have gone too far. When we use stereotypes, we take in the gender, the age, the color of the skin of the person before us, and our minds respond with messages that say hostile, stupid, slow, weak. Those qualities aren't out there in the environment. They don't reflect reality."[6]

Bigoted thinking, and the actions that result from it, reflects the notion that a person's characteristics are more important than his or her character. A bigoted person judges individuals negatively on the basis of traits such as skin color or religion, rather than on the basis of actual character. A bigot also draws unfavorable conclusions about entire groups of people based on their single shared trait, such as skin color, nationality, or religion.

Distorted "truths"

Although bigotry is fairly easy to define, people disagree about the nature of bigotry, and whether particular attitudes or actions reflect bigotry. One reason for this conflict is that stereotypes frequently contain a kernel of truth. That kernel is distorted to support prejudice.

For example, just as a hiker in the forest survives by "stereotyping" all bears as potentially dangerous, a female city dweller out for a stroll at night may also attempt to use categories to preserve her safety. Perhaps she has seen photographs on the news of men who have been arrested for assaulting women out alone at night. If the men were all young, African American (perhaps reflecting the population of the city), and wearing baggy clothes and knit caps, then the city dweller out for a walk might categorize every young African American male she sees wearing baggy clothes as a potential mugger. After all, it is true that the criminals she saw on television were black and wearing baggy clothes.

When this woman goes to work the next day in her job in a jewelry store, she may then apply that same categorization, or stereotype, to young African American men who come in to her store. Are they potential customers or potential criminals? Perhaps she calls the security guard as a precaution, although she would not do the same if a young white man in baggy clothes were to walk in to the store. Is the woman a bigot because she harbors fears and suspicions about young black men whom she does not know personally, based on their skin color, age, and manner of dress? Some people would say she is engaged in bigoted thinking, because she has taken a nugget of information about some members of a group—that some young black men in baggy clothes have attacked women at night—and applied it to all members of that group, concluding that all young black men in baggy clothes are suspicious. Others would argue that the woman is justified in judging all young black men in baggy clothes negatively, because at least some of them are criminals, and she is only being cautious. This is how people who use stereotypes defend their prejudices as based in fact; they assert that the kernel of truth applies to a broader group of people than is actually the case.

As another example, Asian Americans sometimes have to deal with the stereotype that they are not loyal U.S. citizens. This stereotype is based in part on the historical fact that Asians were wartime enemies of the United States at least

Japanese POWs during World War II. Because Asians have been frequent wartime enemies of the United States, some people have drawn the stereotypical conclusion that Asian Americans are not loyal U.S. citizens.

three times in the twentieth century: during World War II (Japan), the Korean conflict (North Korea), and the Vietnam War (North Vietnam). Alice Young, now a lawyer, told a reporter about the day her class in a McLean, Virginia, school watched a movie in the early 1960s:

> They had a film on communism, and we were all sitting in our chairs watching it, and the communist happened to be a Chinese-looking person, and at the end of the film, it said if you see anyone who looks suspicious, please call your FBI bureau. And the lights came on, and all of a sudden I noticed that all my classmates had moved their chairs away from me.[7]

Alice Young was not a communist or an enemy of the United States. But she was Asian, and some Asians are communists or have been wartime enemies of this country. From that kernel of truth, some people draw the conclusion that Asian people generally are not to be trusted as loyal Americans, even though that conclusion is not supported by facts.

Preference or prejudice?

Another reason the nature of bigotry is subject to debate is that attitudes and actions that some view as bigoted, others defend as personal preferences. As Dr. Wilhelmina Leigh of the Joint Center for Political and Economic Studies in Washington, D.C., told a 2000 conference on the nature of race-based bigotry, or racism,

> It is sometimes very difficult to separate what is a racist action or racist behavior from what is simply the expression of preferences in the marketplace. . . .

> For instance, if you think about the market for shoes, and let's say that the only color shoes that are sold are either green or pink. And everybody who buys shoes does not like pink. They like green. So all the pink shoes stay in the stores and all the green shoes go home with people. Now is that racist? Are we discriminating against the pink shoes, or is this simply an expression of preference? It's necessary, but difficult, to figure out what's really going on.[8]

The difference between an innocent preference and racism may lie in the type of judgments or conclusions drawn by the person expressing the preference (or the racism). In expressing a preference for green shoes, one is not attacking the character of pink shoes. One is not saying that pink shoes are inherently inferior. An individual's preference for green shoes allows for the possibility that another person may prefer pink. In contrast, racial bigotry reflects a judgment that people of color are inherently inferior to white people. This judgment is not presented as a matter of opinion or preference but as a matter of fact. But the "fact" underlying bigotry is misinformed; it is based on stereotype rather than reality.

The spectrum of bigotry

The nature of bigotry is also complicated by the broad range of behavior that is included in the concept. Bigotry is a continuum that runs the gamut from words to action, from jokes or pranks to deadly force.

American society has traditionally been hesitant to condemn words or ideas, no matter how hurtful. Yet many believe that bigoted words and ideas have effects as real as blows in a fistfight, and can lead to or encourage more dangerous bigoted actions. If the expression of bigoted words represents one point on the spectrum of bigoted behavior, another point is represented by bigotry-inspired exclusion of other people or denial of opportunity. This can happen at work, in the marketplace, at school—in just about any setting. Beyond exclusion and denial of opportunity lie harassment and, at the extreme end of the spectrum, life-threatening violence.

Two grisly incidents in 1998 focused public attention on the problem of bigotry-inspired violence in America. First was the murder of forty-nine-year-old James Byrd Jr., whose attackers tied the African American man alive to the back of their pickup truck and dragged his body along a bumpy country road. Byrd was found dead in the woods in Jasper, Texas, missing his head and right arm. A few months later came the beating death of Matthew Shepard in Laramie, Wyoming. Shepard was a twenty-one-year-old openly gay student at the University of Wyoming. His attackers pistol-whipped him and tied him to a fence outside of town, leaving him in freezing temperatures. A passerby found Shepard

John William King (center) grins as he is led from the courthouse after being sentenced to death for the gruesome murder of an African American man, James Byrd Jr.

eighteen hours later, and the young man died in a hospital five days later.

Bigotry not only takes many forms, it also targets many groups. In the United States, bigotry is often directed at certain national or ethnic groups, such as people of Hispanic, Native American, or Asian heritage. Homosexuals are also frequently the targets of bigoted action and words. According to government statistics, in recent years the greatest growth rate in hate crimes—that is, criminal acts that are motivated by bigotry—has been against homosexuals and Asians.

But two of the most enduring and powerful patterns of prejudice target African Americans and Jews. The history and ongoing persistence of these prejudices provide insights into the nature of bigotry and its stubborn hold on many Americans.

Slavery's legacy

Racism toward African Americans is inseparable from the history and legacy of slavery in the United States. By the early 1600s, African slaves were brought to the English colonies in North America, which subsequently became the United States. Slavery became particularly entrenched in the South, which depended on slave labor for its plantation economy.

Slaves were considered property, which could be owned, traded, sold, and otherwise managed by their white owners—like livestock. Some whites viewed slaves as less than human. According to Professor David Pilgrim, who founded a museum of racism in Big Rapids, Michigan,

> During slavery the dominant caricatures of Blacks . . . portrayed them as childlike, ignorant, docile, groveling, and, in general, harmless. These portrayals were pragmatic and instrumental. Proponents of slavery created and promoted Black images that justified slavery and soothed White consciences. If slaves were childlike, for example, then a paternalistic institution where masters acted as quasi-parents to their slaves was humane, even morally right.[9]

The end of slavery after the Civil War changed the dominant stereotype of black people. According to the new stereotype, without the restraining effects of slavery, blacks were

Slaves transport rice on a Southern plantation. Racism in the United States has deep roots in slavery, which allowed blacks to be treated as property that could be bought, sold, and traded.

savage and criminal. Popular white writers such as Thomas Nelson Page complained that the slaves of the old days had given way to blacks who were "lazy, thriftless, intemperate, insolent, dishonest, and without the most rudimentary elements of morality." [10]

At the same time that the new black stereotype was being popularized, the Ku Klux Klan, formed by a group of men in December 1865, came to prominence in the South. The Klan, or KKK, engaged in terror and intimidation against African Americans, gaining support from Southerners who were fearful and angry at the emancipation of blacks. The KKK's signature was a burning cross—meant to symbolize white Christian supremacy—left at the site under attack. Klan members carried out their rampages dressed in white sheets and hoods that covered their faces.

Often, the Klan's purpose was to prevent blacks from exercising their newly won right to vote in elections and to hold public office. Sometimes, the goal was to punish blacks who were perceived as somehow disrespectful of white people, particularly white women. Lynching—public murders, generally by hanging from a tree or by shooting, often involving disfigurement and torture—was a form of punishment meted out against blacks by the KKK and by other white mobs. By the late 1860s, the Klan had thousands of members, including leading members of white society such as newspaper editors, political leaders, and ministers.

Black Codes

The KKK lost power and prestige by 1900, as some people objected to the group's bloody methods. But by then, the spread of antiblack sentiment and violence had achieved its intended effects. African Americans rarely voted in elections in the South, and the whites who came into power passed laws that created a segregated society. African Americans were banned from schools, restaurants, train stations, hotels, theaters, restrooms, public parks, swimming pools, and other public facilities used by whites.

These segregation rules, the Black Codes, were also known as "Jim Crow" laws. (The name came from a demeaning char-

acter, Jim Crow, invented by a white minstrel performer in 1828.) A typical example was Section 369 of Birmingham, Alabama's original segregation rules, which stated, "It shall be unlawful to conduct a restaurant . . . at which white and colored are served in the same room."[11]

Jim Crow laws affected nearly every aspect of life in the South, and they strictly limited interaction between whites and blacks. Throughout the Jim Crow states, signs declaring "Whites Only" or "No Coloreds" marked water fountains, entrances and exits, and public facilities. Blacks were not permitted in white hospitals, prisons, schools, churches, cemeteries, or public restrooms. Sometimes there were separate facilities for African Americans—but not always. An African American family traveling by car in the South might have to drive many miles between restaurants or restrooms.

Signs like this were common in the South, where Jim Crow laws segregating blacks and whites severely limited interaction between the races.

Murder in Mississippi

Jim Crow continued to be a mainstay of life in many southern states until the 1960s. No single event led to the demise of the system. Rather, a number of events seemed to

Fourteen-year-old Emmett Till was kidnapped, tortured, and murdered for flirting with a young white woman in 1955. His attackers were found innocent by an all-white jury.

awaken the nation to the consequences of segregation and white mob justice. One was the 1955 murder of a fourteen-year-old African American boy, Emmett Till. Emmett was from Chicago, visiting relatives in Mississippi. As a young Northerner, Emmett may not have known about the many unwritten rules of the Jim Crow South, including the rules barring black men from making any disrespectful or familiar remarks to white women.

After Emmett flirted with a pretty twenty-one-year-old white woman, he was kidnapped, tortured, and murdered by the woman's husband and another man. An all-white jury found the murderers innocent of any wrongdoing, and they were set free. But newspapers and magazines from around the country covered the story, and people became more aware of the injustices of racism.

In the years that followed, racists unleashed more violence against blacks, particularly against blacks who dared to demonstrate or take action against the Jim Crow system. Sometimes the violence was committed by white police officers or other law enforcement officials. In May 1963, for example, officers in Birmingham, Alabama, turned powerful fire hoses—strong enough to blast the bark off trees—on adults and children who were peacefully demonstrating to end segregation in the city's public facilities and stores. On September 15, 1963, white supremacists bombed the Sixteenth Avenue Baptist Church in Birmingham, killing four black girls who were there for Sunday school. As these and other events were broadcast around the nation on the nightly news, many white people grew disgusted with and ashamed of the fruits of bigotry.

The rise of civil rights

Although demonstrators succeeded in getting some southern cities and communities to integrate schools and other facilities, the successes were piecemeal. In 1964, President Lyndon Johnson (himself a Southerner) signed into law the

Civil Rights Act of 1964, which overturned the Jim Crow system. The law prohibited race discrimination in public accommodations, from schools to restaurants, and in employment. But African Americans were still not allowed to exercise their right to vote in the South. The Reverend Martin Luther King Jr. and other civil rights activists organized demonstrations to demand the right to vote. Many white people, including government officials, opposed the demonstrators with force.

The turning point was March 7, 1965. On that day, which became known as "Bloody Sunday," black activists marching in support of voting rights from Selma to Montgomery, Alabama, were attacked by Alabama police and sheriffs. Seventeen African Americans were hospitalized as a result of the attack, which was broadcast on national television. Millions of Americans were appalled.

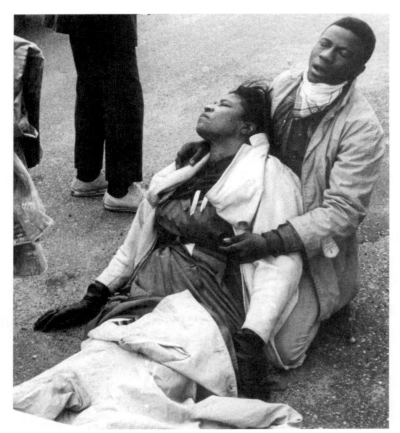

A protester suffering from exposure to tear gas supports an unconscious woman during the "Bloody Sunday" civil rights march, which led to passage of the Voting Rights Act in 1965.

On March 15, President Johnson made a speech to the United States Congress to ask for passage of a voting rights bill. He said,

> As a man whose roots go deeply into Southern soil I know how agonizing racial feelings are. I know how difficult it is to reshape the attitudes and the structure of our society.
>
> But a century has passed, more than a hundred years, since the Negro was freed. And he is not fully free tonight. . . .
>
> The time of justice has now come. I tell you that I believe sincerely that no force can hold it back. It is right in the eyes of man and God that it should come. And when it does, I think that day will brighten the lives of every American. [12]

By August 6, 1965, the Voting Rights Act was the law of the land. The effect was dramatic. African Americans registered to vote, and they started to vote in elections. In 1964, there were seventy-nine black elected officials in the South and three hundred in the entire nation. By 1998, there were nine thousand elected black officials across the nation, including six thousand in the South.

Persistent racism

Yet the legacy of slavery, segregation, and years of prejudice endures. In 1998, of 4,321 crimes in which the victims were targeted because of their race, 2,901—or 67 percent—of the incidents were against blacks. Yet blacks account for only 12 percent of the U.S. population. Moreover, African Americans continue to be targets of bigotry and discrimination in the workplace, in restaurants and stores, and elsewhere.

Race-based violence also persists. Only a few years ago, in a crime that was eerily reminiscent of the murder of Emmett Till, another African American teenager fell victim to a beating by a group of young white men. This time, however, the setting was not the South—it was Chicago, Illinois. On March 21, 1997, thirteen-year-old Lenard Clark and two friends made the mistake of riding their bikes from their apartment complex in Chicago's South Side—a poor high-rise black ghetto—to Bridgeport, historically a white neighborhood. When three older white teenagers surrounded the boys, Lenard's friends escaped, but Lenard did not get away. The three young white men slammed Lenard's head into a wall and beat him into a coma. During the attack, they laughed and yelled racial insults. Then they went home and bragged about what they had done.

Lenard spent weeks in a rehabilitation hospital and suffered brain damage. His attackers managed to elude harsh punishment. Two of them pleaded guilty and were ordered to serve thirty months' probation (which does not involve jail time) and to perform community service. The third went to trial and was convicted in 1998 of aggravated assault. His sentence was eight years in prison.

Ancient roots

Like racism, anti-Semitism—that is, prejudice against Jewish people—has deep roots in society. Although the United States has no official religion, it is (and historically has been) predominantly a Protestant nation. Even in the early days of the nation's history, American Jews were aware that their place in such a Christian society was potentially insecure. Members of the Touro Synagogue in Newport, Rhode Island, went so far as to write a letter to George Washington, the country's first president, expressing their fears. In 1790 Washington responded, writing, "For happily the Government of the United States, which gives to bigotry no sanction, to persecution no assistance, requires only that they who live under its protection should demean themselves as good citizens."[13]

Despite these assurances, anti-Jewish sentiment has always been a fact of life in American society, as in other nations of the world. Prejudice against Jews dates from ancient times, when Jewish people rejected the pagan religions of the ancient Greek and Roman empires. Later, anti-Semitism was spurred by the spread of Christianity and its adoption by the monarchs of Europe; Jewish people again resisted the religion that had become dominant in their communities. In some countries, Jews were forced to live in ghettos, or separate communities shut off from the surrounding towns. Life in these ghettos was often difficult and impoverished.

But even where Jews were integrated into society, they frequently became targets of bigotry, excluded from many institutions and opportunities. Until the second half of the 1900s, for

Henry Ford Sr., founder of the Ford Motor Company, owned a Michigan newspaper that propagated anti-Semitic views in the 1920s.

example, many private schools in the United States—from high schools to law schools to medical schools—admitted only a small number of Jewish students into their classes. Until around the same time, many neighborhoods were closed to Jews (and African Americans). Today, some country clubs and other social groups are still closed to Jewish people or have limits on how many Jews are allowed.

Twisting history

Like blacks, Jews have been subject to negative stereotypes that feed bigotry. Many of these stereotypes have endured for decades and even centuries. For example, a long-entrenched stereotype is that Jews engage in sharp business practices and control the financial world. This stereotype is riddled with fallacies, but like many stereotypes, it sounds as if it could be true, and therefore is difficult to combat.

In fact, Jews historically have been merchants and business-people because they were excluded from other professions. Bigoted thinking twists this historical fact into the notion that Jews have undue influence in the world of finance and banking and, by extension, in the political realm. For example, Henry Ford Sr., who founded the Ford Motor Company, was active in spreading anti-Semitic ideas in the 1920s. He owned a Michigan newspaper, the *Dearborn Independent*, which published many articles maligning Jewish people. These articles were then collected in a four-volume set of books titled *The International Jew*. The books were widely published in English and other languages and even today are easily found on the World Wide Web.

The International Jew portrays all Jews as plotting together to take over the planet. According to this view, Jews plan "to control the world, not by territorial acquisition, not by military aggression, not by governmental subjugation, but by control of the machinery of commerce and exchange." Furthermore, *The International Jew* charges,

> It is not merely that there are a few Jews among international financial controllers; it is that these world-controllers are *exclusively Jews.* . . .Whichever way you turn to trace the harmful streams of influence that flow through society, you come upon a group of Jews. [14]

Henry Ford later apologized to individual Jews and to Jews as a group. After his death in 1947, his company became a publicly owned corporation that engages in projects serving the public interest and supporting Jewish charities. But the prejudice and bigoted thinking reflected in *The International Jew* has endured.

Holocaust denial

The list of anti-Semitic charges is long, but none has been more painful to Jews in recent years than the claim that the Holocaust never happened. According to this view, Nazi Germany was not responsible for the extermination of 6 million

Despite massive evidence like this horrific photograph showing victims of a Nazi death camp, there are people who claim that the Holocaust never happened.

European Jews during World War II. Rather, Jews and allies of Jews fabricated a huge lie to gain sympathy for Jewish people. Those who engage in Holocaust denial develop explanations for, or simply ignore, the massive and horrifying evidence of Nazi death camps, gas chambers, and other elements of the Nazi war against the Jews.

Dozens of sites on the Internet are dedicated to Holocaust denial. Some of them attempt to present their conspiracy theories as respectable historical scholarship. Other Holocaust deniers are more blatant in their bigotry, such as this communication, which circulated on an e-mail list of the National Socialist White Peoples Party in July 1996: "Without the Holocaust, what are the Jews? Just a grubby little bunch of international bandits and assassins and squatters who have perpetrated the most massive, cynical fraud in human history."[15]

The problem of anti-Semitism goes beyond the spread of falsehoods about Jews. Anti-Semitism has a violent face as well. In 1998, of 1,390 religion-bias crimes reported by the Department of Justice, 1,081 of the incidents—78 percent—were against Jews. Jews make up 2 percent of the U.S. population.

Despite the persistence of anti-Semitism in the United States, Democratic presidential candidate Al Gore chose a Jewish person, Senator Joseph Lieberman, as his vice presidential running mate in the 2000 election. Gore's choice marked the first time a Jewish person had been tapped to run for the U.S. vice presidency on the ticket of a major political party. Lieberman was not only Jewish but an Orthodox Jew, a member of one of Judaism's more religiously observant groups.

Jews and non-Jews throughout the United States saw this choice as an important milestone in American Jewish history. Still, even the head of the Democratic Party

Senator Joseph Lieberman, the first Jewish vice presidential candidate on the ticket of a major political party.

voiced concerns about the effect of anti-Semitism on the success of the Gore-Lieberman team: "I don't think anyone can calculate the effect of having a Jew on the ticket. If Joe Lieberman were Episcopalian, it would be a slam dunk."[16]

Anti-Semitism and racism are probably less powerful forces in American society today than they were fifty or even twenty-five years ago. But the forces of bigotry are far from extinct. The government of the United States may have made great strides in fulfilling George Washington's promise of giving "to bigotry no sanction, to persecution no assistance." But many people who live in the United States have not fallen into step, so prejudice marches on.

2

The Causes of Bigotry

BIGOTRY IS CAUSED by being human. That may seem like an awfully simplistic explanation for a multifaceted issue, but it sums up the problem in a nutshell: Prejudice, according to many social scientists, is an innate human trait.

Recently, a group of scientists conducted an experiment. In the experiment, white people were shown pictures of other people, both white and black. Then they were shown another set of pictures of only black people (including some whose pictures they had just been shown) and asked to identify individuals whose pictures they had seen. They also were asked to identify individual white people whose pictures they had seen.

What the scientists found was that the whites were much worse at recognizing black faces than at recognizing white faces. The reason for these results, according to Daniel Levin of Kent State University, is that many white people tend to "code" blackness in a way that lumps all black people together. "The problem is . . . [people] substitute group information, or information about the race, for information about the features that help us tell individual people apart,"[17] he said.

Other evidence confirms that human beings have a built-in tendency to size up other people quickly based on a few, often superficial characteristics. Some scientists suggest that this practice stems from early human history, when it was necessary for people to determine quickly whether others were friend or foe based on their tribal or ethnic identity. The tendency of human beings to view the world in terms of "us" against "them" is so commonplace that social scientists have coined theories about it.

For example, the social identity theory explains that people create "in-groups" of which they are members. They compare their in-group to other groups of different people, which they see as "out-groups." In this process, people favor their own group and develop a bias against members of out-groups.

Social identity is only one of several theories that scientists have advanced since the 1950s—in the aftermath of World War II and the Holocaust—to help explain the causes of prejudice and bigotry. Other research suggests that some individuals, particularly those with authoritative or rigid personalities, are more disposed than others to hold prejudices. One theory, backed by research, holds that some people's bigotry is their way of acting out their own psychological conflicts and responding to poor parenting.

Whatever the precise theory advanced to explain the origins of bigotry, the practice of judging others based on incomplete information about them is a deeply ingrained tool in human relations. This is a double-edged tool, because while stereotyping can help people engage in interactions without the need for exhaustively examining others, it can easily lead people to wrong and unfair conclusions. The psychological and sociological underpinnings of bias indicate how very difficult bigotry is to overcome. After all, in a way, prejudice is a normal and powerful part of the human condition.

Role models

To say that prejudice is an unavoidable element of the human mind-set is not the end of the conversation about the causes of bigotry. People are capable of seeing beyond their innate preference for their own group to appreciate the value of others. If innate prejudice were the only cause of bigotry, then bigotry might well be on its way toward extinction. But a range of other factors also contribute to bigotry.

For example, children may be born with the innate human tendency to categorize and stereotype but probably not with the acquired human tendency to hate. Bigotry often begins at home, with lessons learned from parents. As one young person said in the book *Hate Hurts*, "He [another child] told me, 'My mother said I can't trust black people. I'm supposed to

A small child poses with his parents in Ku Klux Klan robes in 1949. Bigoted views are often learned from one's parents during childhood.

hate black people.'"[18] Lessons learned at home can influence a person beyond young childhood. Clinton Sipes engaged in violent racism from the age of fourteen until he was twenty-one. He said he became a white supremacist and active member of the Ku Klux Klan by following the example of his grandfather:

> It's hard to know the right thing to do when you've got no education, no vocational training and you've got small support. I grew up in a predominantly white area. My grandfather was involved with the KKK in the 30's. That's when I first experienced any white supremacist activities, when I visited my grandfather in Galveston, Texas.[19]

Even if parents are perfect role models, others—friends, teachers, television, and other media—influence children. For example, although many teachers and students work to promote understanding and acceptance among different groups, schools can be cauldrons of prejudice. In September 1999 the Gay, Lesbian, and Straight Education Network (GLSEN) released a survey on school climate. Ninety-one percent of gay and lesbian students polled in thirty-two states said they heard words like *faggot, dyke,* and *queer* regularly at school. Sixty-nine percent experienced direct verbal harassment. Twenty-four percent reported suffering physical harassment.

More than one-third of the students polled in the GLSEN survey also said that the offensive remarks were made by faculty or staff at their schools, not by fellow students, and that other students were more likely than adults to try to help stop the harassment. In response to these findings, Judy Shepard, whose son Matthew was killed in 1998 by two gay-bashing assailants, said,

> I sort of get the feeling that teachers and administrators feel that they grew up with that teasing in school, and they made it through—they treat it almost as a rite of passage. We survived it, you can survive it. This is how you grow. Oh, ignorant people! Kids have scars—from being teased because they had big ears. What kind of scars do they have from being teased because they're black, or gay?[20]

A man protests against homosexuality at the trial for the killers of Matthew Shepard, a young gay man who was killed because of his sexual orientation.

Peer pressure

Another way prejudice is fostered in school is through peer pressure. The problem is not so much classmates pressuring one another to be bigots but, rather, pressure to conform to stereotypes. In many schools, particularly high schools, there is a way to "act black" and a way to "act white." When, for example, some African American students insist that other African Americans act in a way that they deem acceptable for blacks—or suffer the consequences, such as teasing, exclusion, or worse—they are perpetuating stereotypes.

Recently, high school teacher Patrick Welsh talked to high school athletes to understand why there were "black" and "white" sports. When senior Alicia Hopkins at T. C. Williams High School in Alexandria, Virginia, began playing soccer and softball in elementary school, other black girls mocked her. Hopkins, who is black, explained, "They'd come up and ask me, 'Why are you playing those white sports?' They'd call me a sellout. For me, mixing with white girls is normal. But black friends don't like it. Because I use proper speech . . . I'm not 'black enough' for them."[21]

Such pressures to conform may lead to two results, which have a domino effect on prejudice. First, some black students may buckle under to pressures to "act black" and curtail their achievements. By perpetuating the stereotype that blacks are not as smart as whites, these black students thus feed the bigoted idea that blacks are inferior to whites. Moreover, black students themselves may, consciously or unconsciously, accept this notion. Economist Thomas Sowell explains:

> Once, while teaching an all-black class at Howard University, I asked them to imagine what would happen if a black child in the middle of the ghetto were born with brain cells identical to those with which Einstein entered the world.

> There was much interesting speculation, but not one person in that room thought that this child would grow up to be another Einstein. If he were born to a teenage mother in a gang-infested area, he might be lucky to grow up at all—and he might well be one of those conditioned to believe that putting his efforts into academic work would be "acting white."[22]

White people often stereotype blacks based on their perceptions of the world around them, a world in which blacks often occupy a lower economic and social status than whites.

Lessons learned

Sometimes the lessons children learn about prejudice come not from parents, peers, or mentors but from their observations about the world around them. In *The First R: How Children Learn Race and Racism*, a book published in 2001, two sociology professors studied the racial attitudes of fifty-eight children at a racially diverse urban preschool. Although teachers there taught an antibias curriculum, children as young as three and four exhibited racist tendencies. The book opens with a three-year-old white girl moving her cot at rest time. "I can't sleep next to a nigger," she said. "Niggers are stinky." Later on the playground, a four-year-old says to another, "Get off, white girl! Only black folks on the swing, you see?"[23]

The authors acknowledge that such remarks are learned from others, but they see something else at work. These young children, they say, are interpreting the world as they see it—a world in which white people have money and prestigious jobs and black people are more likely to be lower on the economic totem pole:

Who mops the floors at school? Who bags the groceries? Who digs the ditches and mows the lawns? . . . Generally speaking, whites and people of color do not occupy the same social space or social status, and this very visible fact of American life does not go unnoticed by children. [24]

Other studies also show that when one group (such as white people) does better economically than another group (such as black people), prejudice between the two groups often develops. Members of the economically disadvantaged group may believe that the advantaged group has rigged the social and economic system against them. Conversely, members of the advantaged group may think that those in the poorer group do not work hard enough or lack the talents to achieve greater wealth and social standing.

Similarly, the very structure of American society—in which many poor people, particularly people of color, tend to

Poor urban neighborhoods have high crime rates, a fact which leads some outsiders to unfairly characterize all people who live in such areas as criminal and inferior.

live in poor urban neighborhoods—makes it easy to confuse skin color and poverty with inferiority and even criminality. This is because much crime occurs in poor urban areas, and outsiders sometimes equate those who live in poverty with the criminals who operate in those areas. One recent study illustrates this problem. Based on interviews with more than thirty-five hundred employers, University of Massachusetts professor Chris Tilly found that

> Employers' perceptions of particular neighborhoods . . . are confounded with racial stereotypes. There are a lot of negative views that managers hold of the inner city as a place to do business. In about 60 percent of the businesses we surveyed, somebody reported that they were concerned about crime in the inner city. Nearly as many (57 percent) businesses said they were concerned about workforce quality. Now . . . there is an element of reality. There are issues of crime, there are issues of workforce preparedness in the inner city, but it appears that employers exaggerate this.[25]

Media influences

Many people who are concerned about bigotry in society feel that influential institutions such as the media (television, magazines, radio, and Internet sites) help create or perpetuate prejudice in American society. For example, in 2000, an online cartoon site, *Icebox.com*, introduced "Mr. Wong." The character was a yellow-skinned, narrow-eyed, buck-toothed houseboy who pronounced "l" like "r" and was otherwise a bumbler. Many Asian Americans complained that Mr. Wong reflected, and perpetuated, racist stereotypes.

One of the show's opponents, Karen Narasaki, said to a reporter in July 2000, "What does it say about the perception of Asian-Americans that they thought this had the potential to be a hit?"[26] Icebox executives defended the show, saying that it was funny and that they believed in creative freedom. (By early 2001, the Icebox site had become inactive due to financial problems, and "Mr. Wong" was discontinued.)

Some also hold television responsible for perpetuating negative racial stereotypes. One critic, Paul Farhi of the *Washington Post*, concluded that television "reality" shows

William Collins, a former member of the New Black Panther Party for Self-Defense, talks about being voted off the Big Brother *television show. Reality television shows have been criticized for perpetuating negative racial stereotypes.*

feature a character he calls the "Bad Black Guy." According to Farhi's analysis of shows such as *Temptation Island, Survivor, Big Brother,* and *The Real World*, African American men nearly always play "rogues and rascals, bad dudes and playas" in reality shows. He concedes that the shows would not provide entertainment if all the characters were choirboys and Boy Scouts. His complaint is that white people on the shows come in all types—"some noble, some petty, some strong, some weak"[27]—but the African American men are nearly all the same, behaving badly.

One reason this stereotyping happens, Farhi believes, is that generally there is a single token black man on the shows, so that one person seems to represent his whole race. Farhi quotes Harvard University professor of psychiatry Alvin Pouissant: "If you only have one, it causes the audience to generalize. If you have two or three or four personalities, it's hard to stereotype. This is the psychological effect of tokenism. You're supposed to represent the whole race."[28]

Talk radio "shock jocks" also use racial and ethnic stereotypes to entertain and amuse listeners. Don Imus, host of "Imus in the Morning," a nationally syndicated radio show that combines political commentary with satire and comedy, is one example. Imus has called a Jewish reporter a "beanie-wearing Jew boy," and he jokingly excused serial killer Andrew Cunanan, who murdered gay men, because "he's just whacking off freaks."[29] Imus has told reporters that he only means to be funny.

Closet racism

Mainstream news media, such as broadcast and cable news networks, are rarely as blatant as edgy new websites, reality shows, and talk radio. But some observers have found that even respected news media perpetuate bigotry through methods that media expert Av Westin calls "closet racism." In a handbook written for journalists and journalism students,

Controversial radio host Don Imus regularly uses racial and ethnic stereotypes for entertainment purposes on his talk radio show.

Westin quotes newsroom executives who admitted that race bias affects television journalism. "The conventional wisdom among many assignment editors is that white viewers will tune out if blacks or Latinos are featured in segments," Westin said. He quotes one news executive as saying, "My bosses have essentially made it clear: 'We do not feature black people [as on-camera experts].' Period. I mean, it's said. They actually whisper it, 'Is she white?'"[30]

Some claim that the news media exhibit prejudice toward their coverage of certain national groups as well. For example, Sam Husseini, an official with the American-Arab Anti-Discrimination Committee, has argued that when Arab Americans and American Muslims are the victims of discrimination or hate crimes, the media downplay those incidents. At the same time, the media are quick to identify the Arabic or Muslim background of some terrorists and other criminals. Such unbalanced coverage feeds into Americans' bigotry toward Arab Americans and Muslims.

No matter what the influences are that lead a person to develop bigoted ideas, bigotry is generally the result of a search for simple answers in a complex world. The influences that promote bigotry—whether peer pressure, parental example, talk radio, or something else—tend to suggest quick and easy conclusions to difficult problems in that person's life or in society as a whole. If one loses a job, it is the fault of those people from that foreign country. If one's life is made hard because of personal or family problems, it is at least in part because those people with darker skin have spoiled things. Rather than thoroughly analyzing a problem—such as one's own economic hardship or why certain neighborhoods harbor more crime than others—a person may simply heap the blame on others who are different. The factors that lead a person to take this route represent landmarks on the road map to bigotry.

3

Living with Bigotry

BIGOTRY TOUCHES JUST about every aspect of life. It affects how successful a person is at work and where he or she buys the clothes to wear to work. It can determine what neighborhood a person lives in and how neighborly a welcome the family next door extends. From large roadblocks to more trivial annoyances, bigotry is a recurring feature on the American landscape.

Even the more superficial effects of bigotry are significant in their own way. They usually point to a deeper problem of prejudice. "My son Cedric and I were at a department store looking at watches," a Dallas woman told writer Roger Campbell.

> He wanted a good one for his corporate sales job. When my son asked to see a watch, [the salesperson] asked if we were aware of how much it cost. . . .
>
> I guess she thought we were wasting her time. . . . So my son politely asked for another salesperson and bought a nice watch. [31]

As Campbell wrote in an article in *Essence* magazine, this mother was convinced that, "though her [twenty-three-year-old] son spoke and dressed well, the saleswoman assumed he didn't have the money because he was Black." For Campbell, this conclusion rang true. He observed, "Police stop brothers for driving while Black. Suspicious clerks follow them around (for shopping while Black). Taxi drivers pass them by on urban streets (for standing while Black)." [32]

It is entirely possible that the department store salesperson snootily asked every customer, no matter their race, whether they were aware of how much her watches cost. But enough

41

people have observed the racial stereotyping that Cedric, his mother, and Campbell believed was at work in that department store to give rise to the sardonic "Living While Black" line. That is, black people receive less favorable treatment than white people when doing everything from driving to shopping to standing around because they inescapably do whatever they do "while black."

Beyond rudeness

The issue of less favorable treatment in everyday life goes beyond mere rudeness by department store clerks. One of the more infamous cases in recent years involved six black Secret Service agents who were denied service at a Denny's restaurant in 1993. While they sat, deliberately unattended, a group of white Secret Service agents were served. When lawyers for the Secret Service agents sued, they found that race discrimination pervaded the restaurant chain. For example, in a court

After six black Secret Service agents sued Denny's restaurant in 1993 for race discrimination, lawyers found that incidences of bias were rampant in the restaurant chain.

document, a white waitress who worked at several Denny's in California reportedly said that the use of the terms "nigger," "them," "those people," and "that kind" were "not uncommon." The waitress said, "I was told by management that we did not want to encourage black customers to stay in the restaurant."[33]

Another white witness said that at a Denny's he managed in San Jose, employees "routinely" closed the restaurant when "they were concerned about the number of black customers" coming in. "'Black' was used by Denny's management to refer to a situation where too many black customers were in the restaurant,"[34] he said.

Pattern of discrimination

Everyday experiences of bias are fairly commonplace. Recently, for example, the U.S. Department of Justice charged the Adam's Mark Hotel chain with a pattern of discrimination, including overcharging black guests for inferior rooms and subjecting them to stricter security requirements. One of the incidents challenged in the lawsuit involved the Adam's Mark Hotel in Daytona Beach, Florida. When Brenna Graham, a twenty-four-year-old black elementary school teacher from Maryland, checked into the hotel there for the April 1999 Black College Reunion, a desk clerk snapped an orange band around her wrist, identifying her affiliation with the reunion group. The white couple in front of her in line were not asked to wear bands, and neither was Graham's white companion. Graham told a reporter, "It was a scarlet letter. I didn't think they should get away with it."[35] The hotel chain's spokesperson said the company's actions were clumsy but not racially motivated.

In another case, in November 1999, the state of Florida settled a lawsuit against a Miami restaurant owner who imposed a 15 percent service charge on two black diners but not on white customers. The explanation given to the black patrons was that "African Americans are known not to tip well."[36] Allison Bethel, a Florida state assistant attorney general who worked on the case and on a related Florida case against Adam's Mark, told *U.S. News & World Report*, "It's not that these businesses are saying, 'You black people, you get out of my [establishment.]' They are saying, 'Come on in, but we're going to rip you off.'" According to Bethel, these incidents are "the new face of discrimination in the new century."[37]

Subtle bias

The "new face of discrimination" is also called *subtle bias* or *institutional racism*. These labels refer to beliefs and practices that are not overtly or blatantly bigoted but reflect hidden negative stereotypes, usually about people of color. Subtle bias or institutional racism is carried out by a wide range of institutions and individuals—from hotels to police departments to employers.

Those who are concerned about subtle bias say that unfair, often unconscious, stereotyping causes police to stop African Americans more than they do whites and causes retailers to suspect black shoppers of being more likely to steal than whites, to name only two of the problems. Others argue that the negative stereotypes are unfortunate but true, and therefore practices based on those stereotypes do not reflect bigotry. The practice known as racial profiling illustrates this debate.

Racial profiling is a practice in which police use race as the basis for deciding which motorists to stop and question for possible criminal wrongdoing. For example, a 1999 investigation found that New Jersey state troopers were much more likely to pull over black or Hispanic drivers than whites on suspicion that they had been involved in criminal activity, solely because of the drivers' race. In 2000, 73 percent of the people stopped and searched by New Jersey state troopers on the New Jersey Turnpike were minorities. In many cases, troopers searched for evidence of illegal drugs on the drivers and in the cars.

Some people defend racial and ethnic profiling as an efficient and sensible tool. Explained writer John Derbyshire in the *National Review* magazine,

> By far the largest number of Americans angry about racial profiling are law-abiding black people who feel that they are stopped and questioned because the police regard all black people with undue suspicion. They feel that they are the victims of a negative stereotype.

They are. Unfortunately, a negative stereotype can be correct, even useful.[38]

Derbyshire cites statistics collected by the U.S. Department of Justice showing that, for example, in 1997, a black American was eight times more likely than a nonblack person to commit a homicide, and victims reported that 60 percent of robberies were committed by blacks. Therefore, concludes Derbyshire,

> A policeman who concentrates a disproportionate amount of his limited time and resources on young black men is going to uncover far more crimes—and therefore be far more successful in his career—than one who biases his attention toward, say, middle-aged Asian women. . . . A racial-profiling ban, under which police officers were required to stop and question suspects in precise proportion to their demographic representation . . . would lead to massive inefficiencies in police work. Which is to say, massive declines in the apprehension of criminals.[39]

Others argue that national crime statistics such as those cited by Derbyshire do not justify racial profiling on highways, airports, or other places. The fact that young black men

Some people argue that police are justified in using racial profiling because of statistics that show that blacks are more likely than whites to commit crimes.

are, on average, statistically more likely to engage in criminal activity does not mean that the black people traveling a particular highway are more likely to be criminals than white people. In fact, according to the New Jersey attorney general, in his study of the racial profiling practices of New Jersey state troopers in 2000, white people were found to carry illegal drugs more often than minorities. Moreover, Derbyshire's reasoning would appear to allow minorities everywhere to be treated as second-class citizens, vulnerable to being detained by police simply because of the color of their skin. Some believe that this result is intolerable in a democratic society, even if it were to lead to the discovery of a few more criminals.

Some civil rights advocates also reject the notion that practices such as racial profiling reflect "subtle bias"—a kinder, gentler version of old-fashioned racism—at all. Wade Henderson, executive director of the Leadership Conference on Civil Rights, told a reporter in 2000 that blatant racism is still alive and well, as evidenced by, among other things, disparate treatment of African Americans in retail stores:

> Most Americans think that the most blatant forms of discrimination and segregation have ended, that we're dealing now with a much more-complex, often more-subtle form of discrimination. Yet incidents like the ones we're discussing now seem to belie that point. They seem to suggest that even the more-blatant forms of discrimination, though not as institutionalized as they once were . . . are still occurring, and I think stand in mockery of the perception that America has become a colorblind nation.[40]

Job troubles

Whether the bigotry that African Americans encounter in their everyday interactions—shopping while black, traveling while black, dining while black—is a new and improved type of bigotry or more of the same old kind does not alter its effects on its targets. Moreover, often no clear line exists between subtle bias and overt bigotry. Nowhere is this more evident than in places of work, where subtle prejudice and blatant bigotry often coexist and overlap. To complicate matters further, it is often difficult to determine whether a racial, ethnic, or religious minority fails to get a good job because of bigotry or because of some other reason. Whatever the exact

Florida senator Daryl Jones holds up a copy of a discrimination lawsuit filed by twenty-three corrections officers in 2000 against the Florida Department of Corrections. Bigotry in the workplace is a common occurrence that stifles job opportunities for minorities.

balance of factors, the main effect of bigotry in the workplace is the denial of job opportunities for members of minority groups.

As University of Illinois professor John Bentacur explained in a report published in 2000, minorities are frequently excluded from the networks and links that lead to good jobs and training. In Chicago, for example, Bentacur found that employers have set ways of recruiting people for jobs, and those ways stifle opportunities for minorities:

> For example, to recruit professionals, [employers] advertised in suburban papers or in places that were mostly accessible to white people. Or employers recruited from their own networks and, therefore, produced white people. For skilled jobs, they usually dealt with unions and that produced mostly white people. And for clerical jobs, employers went to established schools that were also white and that produced white people. [41]

Bentacur did not suggest that the employers in Chicago were consciously bigoted. However, he did not shrink from labeling his findings "racism": "Racism is alive and is producing the same negative impacts on minorities as it did 20 to 30 years ago. Only now, it is veiled, more entrenched and, therefore, more difficult to deal with." [42]

An important barrier to African Americans in the workplace is the negative perception some white employers have about their social skills. Also called "soft" skills—as opposed to "hard" skills, such as technical expertise—these social skills involve getting along with customers and coworkers, motivation, and the willingness to work hard. Since an employer's process of evaluating a potential employee's soft skills is subjective, the use of stereotypes is nearly inevitable. In his studies on minority employment, University of Massachusetts professor Chris Tilly said,

> We found that negative employer perceptions of blacks' "soft skills" are widespread. About 27 percent of the businesses that we interviewed reported negative views of blacks' interaction skills and a majority of businesses expressed some kind of negative view of blacks' motivation. . . .
>
> It is probably safe to say that there is some reality here. Some of the reality is based on the work environment issues. Some of these perceptions reflect cultural gaps—people not knowing how to understand each other and some of it is based on straightforward stereotypes.[43]

Compounding the problem is the job interview, another subjective screening test. In an interview, an employer can easily apply stereotypes to the job applicant. An applicant who looks or talks different from what the employer is used to might be rejected for bigoted reasons. As Professor Tilly said, based on his surveys,

> In the interview, we frequently heard the phrase, "gut feeling." For example, an employer might say, "I got a 'gut feeling' for a worker." And statistically, when the interview was the key screening device for hiring workers, fewer black men get employed. On the other hand, the use of more formal procedures generally increases the hiring of blacks.[44]

Housing discrimination

Bigotry affects not only where members of certain minority groups work but also where they live. In the past, bigoted exclusionary practices in housing were implemented by individual whites who were opposed to black, Jewish, Latino, or other minority newcomers or by "neighborhood improvement associations." White homeowners included special antiminority clauses in the legal documents, called deeds, relating to their property. Such clauses, known as "restrictive covenants," legally bound the homeowners and anyone to whom they sold their houses to refuse to sell to minorities. Courts enforced restrictive covenants until the Supreme Court said they were illegal in 1948 in the case of *Shelly v. Kraemer.*

The passage of time has weakened any continuing effects of the old restrictive covenants. However, according to sociologist Gregory D. Squires, today's housing discrimination reflects the legacy of other practices from the past. For example, real estate agents (licensed professionals who help people buy and sell homes) and housing officials for years followed guidance provided by a 1939 Federal Housing Administration manual, which warned that, "if a neighborhood is to retain stability, it is necessary that properties shall continue to be occupied by the same social and racial classes." [45] Until the 1950s, the National Association of Realtors officially steered clients into certain neighborhoods according to race. In 1989, Urban Institute researchers found that racial steering and

White tenants erected this sign in 1942 to prevent African Americans from moving into their community. Today, housing discrimination is much more subtle, but still exists.

other methods still blocked opportunities for approximately half of all black and Hispanic home seekers nationwide.

The process of obtaining home loans, or mortgages, is also affected by discrimination, and shuts minorities out of home ownership. A home buyer almost always must borrow from a bank or other lender to obtain the money needed to make such a large purchase. A large study published in the *American Economic Review* in 1996 found that, among equally qualified buyers, blacks were rejected for applications to borrow funds with which to buy homes 60 percent more often than whites.

The causes of these rejections are subject to debate. No doubt, some black applicants were rejected for nondiscriminatory reasons, such as not having a job with a sufficient salary to repay the mortgage. But other research suggests that discrimination accounts at least for some of the rejections. In fact, two studies released in September 1999 indicated that things were getting worse instead of better. A study by the Association of Community Organizations for Reform Now (ACORN) found that black and Latino applicants for home loans were rejected much more frequently than white applicants, and the rates of rejection were increasing. A separate study by the Urban Institute analyzed paired testing in which each pair of testers—one minority, one white—gave similar credit histories, incomes, and financial history and asked for the same type of loan. Overall, minorities got less information about loan products, received less time and information from loan officers, and were quoted higher prices in most of the cities in the study.

As these studies indicate, bigotry in housing today involves fairly complex financial practices. Whether intentional discrimination is at work in the denial of a mortgage loan is not always clear. Sometimes members of racial and ethnic minorities are blocked from buying homes simply because they are not financially qualified to obtain a mortgage. But opportunities are also blocked because of prejudice behind closed doors in lending offices and similar institutions.

School failings

Similar questions about hidden bias have arisen in the field of education. In March 2000, the Applied Research Center

(ARC) of Oakland, California, reported that public schools across America fail to provide the same quality of education for students of color as for white students. The ARC study looked at student discipline, dropout rates, access to advanced classes, graduation rates, and other factors in twelve cities from Boston to San Francisco. The study's authors concluded,

> Throughout the nation, public schools subject African American, Latino, and Native American students to a special kind of "racial profiling": on the road to a decent education, students who are brown or black can expect to be pulled over frequently, while their white counterparts whiz on by.

> If the public schools regularly failed to serve students of color in a single aspect of their education, that would be bad enough. What the research reveals, however, is far more pernicious: the cumulative effect upon students of color of an education experience that channels them away from academically challenging courses, punishes them more frequently and more harshly, and ultimately pushes them out of school without a diploma—all in much higher proportions than their white counterparts.[46]

With respect to student discipline, for example, the ARC study found that African American, Latino, and Native American students are suspended or expelled in far greater numbers

Studies have shown that African American, Latino, and Native American students do not receive the same quality of education as whites in public schools across America.

than white students. In one school district in Oregon, the ARC found that Latino students accounted for 10 percent of the student population but 22 percent of suspended or expelled students. According to the study, "In San Francisco, for example, African American students are suspended or expelled at *more than three times* their proportion of the general school population (56% compared to 18%)."[47]

The ARC report did not suggest that school policies are aimed specifically at minority students. Instead, the reason minority students get in trouble more frequently than white students seems to lie in the general nature of school discipline. Deciding whether a student's behavior is serious enough to warrant suspension or expulsion is often a subjective matter, and teachers and administrators may be guided by negative stereotypes about African Americans, Latinos, and Native Americans. The report concluded,

> When discipline codes define punishable behavior in subjective terms, such as "disrespect" or "defiance of authority," how the code is applied often depends on how individual teachers and administrators interpret students' behavior. Too often that interpretation is affected not only by a student's objective behavior but also by differences of race and ethnicity.[48]

Many observers say that because inequalities in education are not the result of intentional discrimination, critiques such as that published by the ARC are not helpful. And in fact, such critiques breed suspicion between different races. Others argue that intent is not important. What is important, they say, is that nothing can justify a society in which millions of minority students receive an education that is inferior to that of white students. That inferiority alone, according to this view, is evidence of institutional racism in the U.S. public schools.

Special ed segregation

New evidence also suggests that racial bias may be at work in the field of special education. In March 2001, Harvard University's Civil Rights Project published reports, based on data concerning 24 million children, that black children are nearly three times more likely than whites to be labeled mentally retarded, and almost twice as likely to be tagged as having emotional problems. These children are then forced into special education classes where progress is slow and trained teachers are in short supply.

One study found that black boys who attend good schools in wealthy white communities are at greater risk of being labeled retarded and put in special classes than those attending low-income, mostly black schools. This raises concerns that administrators and teachers at these wealthier schools move too quickly to get black students out of the mostly white classrooms. The researchers, from Virginia Commonwealth University and East Tennessee State University, said the wealthier schools engaged in "systemic bias" leading the black students to be "labeled mentally retarded inappropriately."[49]

The problem is complex: It is partly about educators classifying black students as a result of racism and partly about educators writing off black students too soon because of academic problems or behavior. The Civil Rights Project's

Evidence has shown that blacks are much more likely than whites to be labeled mentally retarded or as having emotional problems, and to be put into special education classes.

papers also said that assignment to special ed classes may increase a student's chance of getting in trouble with the law and failing state tests used for promotion and graduation purposes. Also, minority children sent to special ed are less likely to be returned to regular classes than similar white children, according to the report. "To the extent that minority students are misclassified, segregated or inadequately served," the researchers concluded, "special education can contribute to a denial of equality of opportunity, with devastating results in communities throughout the nation."[50]

Sinking to stereotypes

Wherever and however bigotry appears, its victims share a common experience: They are deprived of opportunities. But there is another, less commonly understood effect as well: Negative stereotypes have a way of changing the behavior of the people they unfairly characterize.

Psychologists and others have found that, if a person is aware of a stereotype applied to a particular group he or she belongs to, it can affect how well that person does on intellectual and other tasks. Some suggest that this may explain why black students, even those from middle-class families and good schools, often score lower than whites on standardized tests. This testing gap gets wider as students grow older, perhaps because, around sixth grade, race becomes a major factor in social life at school. By around age eleven or twelve, young people become more aware of the group they belong to and stereotypes about that group. Being aware of negative stereotypes—such as "blacks are stupid" or "girls can't do hard math"—and worrying about possibly confirming them may actually cause the targets of the stereotypes to perform worse on the tasks in question.

For example, in a study of forty black and forty white Princeton University undergraduates who volunteered to play miniature golf, some of them were told they were being tested for their "natural ability." Among these, black students scored on average more than four strokes better than white students. The other group was told the study was about "the ability to think strategically." In that group, white students scored four strokes better. One of the psychologists involved, Jeff Stone, said, "When people are reminded of a negative stereotype about themselves—'white men can't jump' or 'black men can't think'—it can adversely affect performance."[51]

The effects of stereotypes and the experience of bigotry, then, are deeply imprinted in American society and its members. Bigotry is most certainly about the loss of opportunity. But, perhaps even more troubling, it is also about the loss of one's ability to be one's best self.

4

Extremes of Bigotry:
Hate Groups and
Hate Crimes

BIGOTRY IS PART of ordinary, everyday life across the United States but its reach goes even further than that. For some people, bigoted thinking is a central principle of their lives. These people may form or join organizations whose very purpose is to promote bigotry. They may encourage, or commit, acts of violence inspired by their bigoted ideas. Although such extreme bigotry is not common, its threat of violence casts a shadow over society. And apart from the threat of violence, the messages spread by people who subscribe to extremely prejudiced ideas alter the climate of American society.

A group that calls itself the National Alliance begins its goals grandly:

> In spiritually healthier times, our ancestors took as theirs those parts of the world suited by climate and terrain to our race: in particular, all of Europe and the temperate zones of the Americas, not to mention Australia and the southern tip of Africa. This was our living area and our breeding area, and it must be so again. We must have White schools, White residential neighborhoods and recreation areas, White workplaces, White farms and countryside. We must have no non-Whites in our living space, and we must have open space around us for expansion. We will do whatever is necessary to achieve this White living space and to keep it White. [52]

Among other things, the National Alliance goals include an overhaul of modern culture in the United States:

> What we must have . . . is a thorough rooting out of Semitic and other non-Aryan values and customs everywhere. In specific terms, this means a society in which young men and women gather to revel with polkas or waltzes, reels or jigs, or any other White dances, but never to undulate or jerk to Negroid jazz or rock rhythms. . . . It means films in which the appearance of any non-White face on the screen is a sure sign that what's being shown is either archival newsreel footage or a historical drama about the bad, old days. [53]

Young people who enjoy rap, or rock, or pop music may find such statements ridiculously quaint or just cranky. The idea that white Aryans—that is, white people of northern European origin—need "White living space" may seem either a very odd idea or an interesting proposition, but in either case, so far-fetched as to be harmless. The notion that in the rosier past, humankind was "spiritually healthier" may seem like wishful thinking or one way of looking at history. And in fact, only a tiny minority of white people in the United States hold the goals and principles of the National Alliance.

But many observers insist that the National Alliance, its ideas, and other like-minded groups are not harmless. According to a report issued in 2000 by the Anti-Defamation League, the National Alliance "is the single most dangerous organized

The Aryan National Alliance is considered a dangerous hate group, and its members have been known to commit violent crimes against people of other races.

hate group in the United States today." The report continues, "In the past several years, dozens of violent crimes, including murders, bombings and robberies have been traced to NA members or appear to have been inspired by the group's propaganda. . . . There has been evidence of NA activity in no fewer than 26 states nationwide."[54]

Groups such as the National Alliance, and hate-inspired violence, occupy the extreme end of the broad spectrum of ideas, people, and behavior that represent bigotry in the United States. Although groups that promote virulent bigotry do not attract large numbers of followers, they can exert influence beyond their absolute numbers in the population. The ideas these groups circulate are often extremely inflammatory and hard to ignore. The threat of violence they pose can upset communities and society at large. Although actual acts of violence inspired by bigotry are also relatively few in number, and are committed by a very small segment of society's fringes, such crimes alter the feel of everyday life in America.

The resilient Klan

Hate groups are organizations formed by bigoted people to promote their brand of bigotry. Although some hate groups are loosely organized and fairly ineffective in spreading their message, others are more powerful and pursue harmful goals, including violence against African Americans, Jews, foreigners, and other minorities.

Perhaps the most well-known and oldest hate group in the United States is the Ku Klux Klan. After being very active in intimidating newly freed slaves in southern states after the Civil War, the Klan, or KKK, fell out of favor even among Southerners because of the horrific violence it supported. By 1915, however, the KKK was revitalized, and its targets expanded to include Jews, Catholics, and immigrants from southern Europe in addition to African Americans. This broadened scope of hate also broadened the KKK's appeal outside of the South.

In the early 1920s the Klan was back to its violent ways, bringing terror to communities through lynchings and cross burnings. The group also gained political power. The KKK's

Thousands of Klansmen and Washington, D.C. citizens watch the burning of an eighty-foot cross by the KKK in 1925.

views on the inferiority of certain ethnic groups were given legal force in the 1924 immigration law. That law set strict limits to keep out Asian and southern European immigrants, and favored immigrants from northern Europe. In the 1950s the Klan increased its strength again, taking advantage of white opposition to the civil rights movement, which was pushing to end segregation in the South. Today, the Klan has splintered into a number of groups, with varying principles and goals. It has also shifted geographically. In the late 1990s, according to the Southern Poverty Law Center, Pennsylvania hosted more public Ku Klux Klan rallies than Alabama.

At the extremes

For some bigots, the Klan is not extreme enough. Two other groups, the National Alliance and the World Church of the Creator, are typical of hate groups that appeal to these people. The National Alliance, the group whose goals include securing "White living space" at the expense of nonwhites, has been led since the 1970s by former Oregon State University physics professor William L. Pierce. Under a pseudonym, Pierce wrote the novel *The Turner Diaries*, published in 1978, which tells of a successful world revolution by an all-white army, and the systematic extermination of blacks, Jews, and other minorities. Some experts believe the book has inspired extremist violence.

A long essay titled "Who Rules America?" is typical of the National Alliance's views. The essay, featured on the National Alliance website, claims that the United States is heavily influenced by an evil Jewish-owned media. It asserts, "The Jewish control of the mass media is the single most important fact of life, not just in America, but in the world today. There is nothing—plague, famine, economic collapse, even nuclear war—more dangerous to the future of our people."[55]

Another group with strong racist and anti-Semitic teachings is the World Church of the Creator, founded by a law

Matt Hale, founder of the World Church of the Creator, a white supremacist group that uses a website to reach children and teenagers.

school graduate named Matt Hale. The World Church of the Creator has several content-rich websites with material aimed specifically at children and teenagers. Like the National Alliance and some other relatively new hate groups, the World Church of the Creator attempts to express its ideas in conversational tones and to suggest that these ideas are nothing less than absolute truths—even based in science. For example, the frequently asked questions (FAQ) section of the main World Church of the Creator Web page explains that the group's beliefs are based on

> The Eternal Laws of Nature. Nature tells each species to expand and upgrade itself to the utmost of its abilities. Since the White Race is Nature's finest achievement and since we encompass the White Race, there can hardly be any other goal that even compares in importance. . . .

> The first prerequisite to our attaining victory is to be completely honest about what we are and what we are not. We are racists because we believe in Race. We are anti-Semites because we oppose the Jews.[56]

The goals of the World Church of the Creator are to protect the purity of the white race, expand the population of the white race, and reduce the presence of Jews and other "mud races."[57]

Building memberships

Hate groups are not simply anonymous entities with websites and position papers. They are people who are drawn together by common beliefs, resentments, or goals. Although people of all ages join hate groups, young adults are particularly likely to join. Such people may be attracted by the sense of belonging and community these groups offer. They have often experienced personal hardship and are therefore susceptible to the hate groups' message that some other group of people is to blame. T. J. Leyden Jr., a former member of a group called White Aryan Resistance, explained how he was recruited when he was fifteen years old and dealing with his parents' divorce. He was angry and lonely. In an interview in 1996 after he renounced his racist views, Leyden said,

> I needed to lash out. . . . They [hate groups] look for young, angry kids who need a family. . . . I thought I was being patriotic. We would drink and fight, try to clean up America that way.[58]

T. J. Leyden Jr. was recruited into the White Aryan Resistance when he was a lonely, angry fifteen year old. He has since renounced his racist views.

Hate groups recruit their members through Internet sites, concerts, dances, social gatherings, "churches," gangs, and clubs. When T. J. Leyden turned twenty-one he joined the Marines. While posted at a base in Hawaii he recruited at least four of his fellow Marines by showing them videos about the White Aryan Resistance and playing them the music of bands whose lyrics preach hatred and violence. Elsewhere, Leyden recruited white junior high students to the White Aryan Resistance. Leyden would ask them, "Shouldn't there be a group for you?"[59] He passed out racial comics and Aryan Resistance leaflets to the teenagers and became affectionately known as "Grandpa" among the younger white supremacists.

Leyden also met his wife through members of his hate group. White supremacist friends helped get the couple together. The couple's social life then revolved around the white supremacy movement.

Other groups, such as the National Alliance, gain new members by hanging signs in prominent places, setting up displays at gun shows, and handing out information in suburban neighborhoods. Some hate groups have recently tried to expand their membership to include more women. As Randy Blazak of Portland State University explained to an online magazine in 1999, "They [the hate groups] need as many bodies as possible. Since more white women are working and therefore being laid off or competing with minorities, there is a growing pool of alienated people to target."[60]

Kathleen Blee, a University of Pittsburgh sociology professor, found that women make up 25 percent of hate group members nationwide but 50 percent of new recruits. One woman, a recruiter for the World Church of the Creator, told a reporter that she had hundreds of women from a wide variety of professions and institutions on her e-mail list. She explained,

> They're sick and tired of the propaganda dished out in their college classrooms, like the Holocaust. They ask me for advice. So I feel like a support system for women who are not necessarily ready to join Creator but are looking for a way to bolster their arguments and debates in classrooms with professors.[61]

To these individuals, hate groups can offer not only an enemy but also fellowship among like-minded people. A *Los Angeles Times* reporter described the August 2000 annual gathering of Aryan Nations, which promotes a white separatist state in the Pacific Northwest:

> [About 100] families camped out in tents under the trees, then gathered at picnic tables for hamburgers and spaghetti. Beer was banned, but clusters of skinhead youths competed in a hammer-throwing competition and played raucous white-power music on the stereos of their pickup trucks. German martial music played over the loudspeaker. . . .
>
> Gathering in . . . [the] Church of Jesus Christ Christian and looking up at a bust of Adolf Hitler, they heard speeches from white supremacist leaders from across the country. . . .
>
> Later that night, as darkness fell over the compound, a towering cross and two giant swastikas were set ablaze, lighting up the meadow with an eerie glow.
>
> "Now that is a beautiful sight," a woman murmured, a baby balanced on one hip. Families lined up to get their pictures taken with the cross burning behind their smiles. A young skinhead from Montana . . . dropped down on one knee, took his girlfriend's hand and asked her to marry him.
>
> Then the meadow erupted in low, human roars: "Sieg heil! White power!"[62]

Culture of hate

Hate groups do more than hold picnics in the woods. They also spread their ideas by creating a culture of their own, with their own publications, music, concerts, flags, clothing, and videos. The National Alliance, for example, broadcasts a weekly radio program, "American Dissident Voices," on short wave and AM stations. It publishes a magazine and operates

National Vanguard Books, which publishes white power comic books aimed at high school students. In 1999, the leader of the National Alliance purchased Resistance Records, a "white power" record label. The label has a website, with downloadable music clips, order forms, and a radio channel. Among the bands whose recordings have been released on Resistance Records are Angry Aryans, Blue-Eyed Devils, Nordic Thunder, and Aggravated Assault. White power music sounds similar to mainstream heavy metal, but with racist, violent

This comic book for high school students, published by the National Alliance, glorifies violence toward minorities.

lyrics: "Kill all the niggers and you gas all the Jews, Kill a gypsy and a coloured, too,"[63] sings the skinhead band Ra-HoWa (short for Racial Holy War).

The World Wide Web has become a key strategy of hate groups that seek to disseminate their message. According to the Simon Wiesenthal Center, the number of websites promoting hate more than doubled from 1999 to 2000, from about fourteen hundred to more than three thousand. In a publication titled *Ten Ways to Fight Hate*, another antibigotry organization, the Southern Poverty Law Center, said it found

> around 500 organized U.S. hate groups, virtually all white supremacists with a handful of black separatist groups. Some are tiny—a handful of men—but armed with a computer, E-mail and a Web site, their reach is immense, their message capable of entering a child's private bedroom.[64]

Bigotry-inspired violence

The connection between the bigoted messages conveyed by hate groups—whether through music, Web sites, or otherwise—and actual acts of bigotry directed at racial, religious, or other minorities is unclear. Probably most followers or admirers of hate groups are not inspired to take violent action. Still, members and sympathizers of these groups have committed serious acts of intimidation and violence against targeted groups or individuals.

For example, in 1998 Ryan Wilson and his Philadelphia neo-Nazi group ALPHA HQ engaged in what a judge later called "a relentless campaign of domestic terrorism"[65] against civil rights worker Bonnie Jouhari and her teenage daughter. Jouhari, who is white, was a fair-housing specialist at the Reading-Berks Human Relations Council in Reading, Pennsylvania, and also the founder and chairperson of the Hate Crimes Task Force for Berks County, Pennsylvania.

In response to Jouhari's efforts to promote integrated housing, Roy Frankhouser, once a "grand dragon" of the Pennsylvania Ku Klux Klan, started shadowing Jouhari. She received threatening phone calls at home. Then Ryan Wilson

White supremacist Roy Frankhouser, a former "grand dragon" of the KKK, was found guilty of harassing a civil rights worker for her efforts to promote integrated housing.

displayed images of Jouhari on his website. The images of Jouhari labeled her a "race traitor" and threatened to lynch traitors "from the nearest tree or lamp post."[66] It also showed an animated picture of her office blown up by explosives. Frankhouser subsequently showed the pictures on his "White Forum" cable television show.

Frightened by this intimidation, Jouhari and her daughter fled their home and moved across the country, to Washington State. They then moved several more times after receiving more threatening telephone calls. Finally, the federal Department of Housing and Urban Development sued Ryan Wilson and Roy Frankhouser for violating the Fair Housing Act of 1968 by engaging in intimidation against Jouhari. In June 2000 a judge ordered Wilson to pay Jouhari and her daughter $1,166,863 to compensate them for their emotional distress and for Jouhari's loss of employment. Frankhouser settled the government's lawsuit against him, agreeing to run fair-housing public service announcements on his cable program.

Other incidents of bigotry by people connected to hate groups have been deadlier. In a highly publicized case in August 1999, Buford O. Furrow Jr. opened fire on a Jewish community center in the San Fernando Valley area of southern California, injuring three children, a teenage camp counselor, and an elderly receptionist. After his rampage at the Jewish community center, Furrow stole a car at gunpoint. As he drove away from the scene of the crime, he saw Joseph Ileto, a mail carrier on his daily route. Furrow stopped the car and pumped nine bullets into Ileto, killing him because he assumed Ileto was Hispanic or Asian. In fact, Joseph Ileto was Filipino.

After Furrow was arrested, he told investigators that he drove to Los Angeles with the specific goal of attacking Jews. He said he hoped his actions would incite more violence against Jews. Investigators determined that Furrow had participated in activities with Aryan Nations and also had ties to an anti-Semitic group called Christian Identity. According to the *Los Angeles Times*, Furrow was photographed at an Aryan Nations compound in Idaho wearing an Aryan Nations uniform. However, Aryan Nations leaders and members condemned Furrow's attacks. In January 2001, Furrow pleaded guilty to several charges and received a sentence of life in prison without the possibility of parole.

Buford O. Furrow Jr., who opened fire on a Jewish community center, later said that he hoped his actions would incite further violence against Jews.

Hate crimes

Buford Furrow committed and pleaded guilty to murder as well as other crimes, including attempted murder and violation of gun laws. His actions are also called *hate crimes*. Generally, hate crimes are acts intended to intimidate and hurt others because of their race, religion, national origin, ethnicity, sexual orientation, or disability. The precise definitions of hate crimes are contained in a wide variety of state and local laws, which vary from state to state. These laws cover bigotry-inspired actions ranging from threatening telephone calls to destruction of property to physical assault.

During 1998, 7,755 hate crimes were reported to the FBI by forty-six states and Washington, D.C. (The FBI compiles the figures under the Hate Crimes Statistics Act of 1990.) Of the 7,755 incidents, 4,321 were motivated by racial bias, 1,390 by religious bias, and 1,260 by sexual-orientation bias. Thirteen people were murdered in 1998 in hate-motivated incidents, most of which were racially motivated. What these numbers mean, according to the Southern Poverty Law Center, is that on average approximately every hour, someone commits a hate crime in America. Every day, eight African Americans, three white people, three gay people, three Jews, and one Latino become hate-crime victims. Every week a cross is burned. Once viewed as a southern problem, today seven out of ten hate crimes occur in the north and west sections of the United States.

Although some perpetrators of hate crimes, such as Buford Furrow, have connections to hate groups, most do not. According to the Southern Poverty Law Center, less than 15 percent of hate crimes can be linked to hate-group members. In its publication *Ten Ways to Fight Hate*, the Southern Poverty Law Center notes

> The majority [of hate crimes] appear to be the work of "freelance" haters, young males who are looking for thrills, or defending some turf, or trying to blame someone for their troubles. Rarely are they acting from deeply held ideology. These young men have adopted the rhetoric of hate groups, however, and they mix stereotypes with a culture of violence. In their minds, certain people are "suitable victims," somehow deserving of their hostility. They attack target groups randomly, choosing whoever is convenient.[67]

The goals of the perpetrators of hate crimes vary. Some hate criminals openly say they wish to incite a race war in the United States. Others attack with no goal beyond hurting people. Whatever the goals of people who commit hate crimes, one thing is clear: Hate crimes make society a scarier and less stable place. And whatever the connection between hate groups and the people who commit hate crimes, both are evidence that extreme bigotry maintains a foothold in American society that will not simply disappear.

5

The Law and Bigotry

To SAY THAT bigotry, even in its extreme forms, is firmly established in American society is not to say that bigotry goes unanswered by society's institutions. People who are motivated by bigotry to commit crimes of violence or intimidation are subject to prosecution under various criminal laws and sometimes under special hate-crimes laws as well. Bigotry-inspired actions that fall short of criminal violations can often also be addressed by legal means, particularly by noncriminal, or civil, lawsuits.

Sometimes, as in the case of criminal prosecution of a person who assaults another out of racial hatred, the legal system's role is clear: to hold the criminal accountable for his or her violent actions. In other instances, such as when an employer engages in blatant discrimination against an employee on account of race, legal remedies exist to give that employee his or her due—such as the raise or promotion that was denied because of bigotry.

In other situations, the purposes and effects of applying legal tools to bigotry are less certain. Legal experts, employers, and antidiscrimination advocates differ on whether antidiscrimination laws should remedy only intentional bigotry or should also apply to institutional, or subtle, bias. People also disagree on issues such as whether employers who have engaged in race discrimination should be required by court order to give hiring preferences to individual members of minority groups who were not the actual targets of the employer's past discrimination. In still other cases, laws are simply ineffective in addressing certain aspects of bigotry, such as bigoted speech.

Prosecuting haters

Probably the least controversial use of the legal system in regard to bigotry is the criminal prosecution of people who commit bigotry-inspired violent crimes. Such crimes are punishable under normal state and federal criminal laws that apply to violence generally, whether or not motivated by bigotry. For example, the two young men who killed Wyoming student Matthew Shepard in 1998 because he was gay were charged with murder and kidnapping under Wyoming law. One of the attackers, Russell Henderson, pleaded guilty to the charges and received two life sentences in a Wyoming prison. The other, Aaron McKinney, went to trial before a state court jury in Laramie, Wyoming. The jury found him guilty of murder, aggravated robbery, and kidnapping, and gave him two life sentences.

Many believe that hate crimes should be subject to laws that provide stiffer punishments than ordinary criminal laws. Some forty states have hate-crime laws, although the exact coverage of the laws varies. Generally, these laws provide enhanced penalties for crimes that fit their definition of hate crimes. If an act that is already a crime—such as assault or kidnapping—is motivated by certain types of bigotry, hate-crime laws allow a judge or jury to impose a tougher sentence than would otherwise apply. For example, under Nevada law, sentences are increased by 25 percent for serious crimes judged to be hate crimes.

The types of motivation that can trigger state hate-crime laws include bias based on race, religion, national origin, gender, or sexual orientation. Not all crimes against the protected groups—whether African Americans or Jewish people or gay people—are hate crimes under these laws. To be classified as a hate crime, the illegal action must have been motivated by the perpetrator's prejudice against the victim.

At the national level, federal law singles out a limited number of hate crimes in limited circumstances for special punishment. For example, bias-motivated criminal acts that occur on federal property such as national parks are covered. Some bigotry-inspired violence that interferes with federally guaranteed rights such as voting is also subject to federal hate-crime laws. However, some people believe that federal

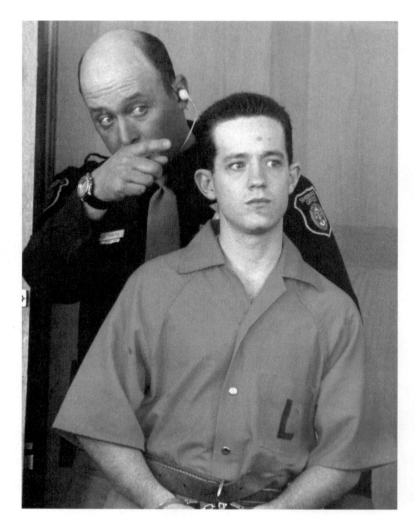

hate-crime laws should be expanded to be tougher on more types of hate crimes in a greater range of settings. Their efforts have led to a heated national debate in the past few years.

Opponents say that an expanded federal hate-crimes law would interfere with the traditional power of the states to punish criminal activities. They also say that, to the extent new federal legislation would address antigay violence, it would give special rights to homosexuals. A related argument is that if federal law makes sexual behavior a federally protected right, then those who object to homosexuality could be prevented from freely exercising their faith and beliefs.

Some people are also concerned about expanding hate-crimes legislation because of the potential effect on the right to free speech. They worry about the fairness of imposing an extra-stiff sentence on a person who uses a racial slur while committing a fairly low-level crime. Although hate-crime laws do not punish people simply for uttering bigoted speech, they do allow judges and juries to consider the speech and state of mind of a criminal who engages in other nonspeech criminal conduct. Some question whether a person's prejudices ought to lead to a more severe criminal punishment than he or she would otherwise have received.

Targeting extremists' wallets

Criminal prosecution is society's way of holding those who commit hate crimes responsible for their violent actions. Government lawyers carry out prosecutions in the name of the state. The victim or survivor of the hate crime receives no tangible compensation beyond the satisfaction of seeing his or her attacker sent to jail.

But many people believe that the most effective way to change harmful behavior is to take aim at the wrongdoer's wallet. This is the approach taken by lawyers who sue hate groups for damages—that is, money—under various civil, or noncriminal, laws. These laws generally were not written with hate crimes in mind, but private lawyers whose clients were victimized by bigotry-inspired violence have nonetheless found the laws useful.

For example, two antibigotry groups, the Southern Poverty Law Center and the Anti-Defamation League, sued the leader of the White Aryan Resistance to hold him responsible for the November 12, 1988, murder of an Ethiopian immigrant by three members of a skinhead gang in Portland, Oregon. The lawsuit claimed that the hate group's leader had incited the gang to murder the immigrant, Mulugeta Seraw, by beating him with a baseball bat. A jury awarded Seraw's family $12.5 million. The lawsuit was not brought under any special law aimed at hate crimes but under Oregon's wrongful death statute, a type of law more often used against doctors or hospitals when their careless or harmful acts result in patients' deaths.

Another major verdict against a hate group was handed down in September 2000. An Idaho jury ordered the white supremacist group Aryan Nations and its founder, Richard Butler, to pay $6.3 million to Victoria Keenan, a Native American woman, and her son Jason. Aryan Nations' security guards had attacked Keenan and her teenage son in July 1998 while the two were driving past the group's guarded twenty-acre compound in rural Idaho, outside Coeur d'Alene. In a separate criminal trial, two of the guards received prison sentences for the attack.

Subsequently, on February 13, 2001, a judge awarded Keenan and her son the Aryan Nations Idaho compound to satisfy the judgment. The compound, with its watchtower, bunkhouses, and prominently displayed swastikas, had been an important gathering place for racists, and the site for an annual Aryan Nations "congress." Among the people who were known to have frequented the compound was Buford

Richard Butler and his white supremacist group Aryan Nations were ordered to pay $6.3 million to a Native American woman and her son after the two were attacked by security guards outside of the Aryan Nations compound.

Furrow, who launched the hate-inspired attack on a Jewish community center in August 1999. With the property no longer in Aryan Nations' hands, according to Victoria Keenan's lawyer, "The immediate social value is that the Buford Furrows will not have this place to learn their hatred and train for it anymore. After this, they're going to have to go somewhere else."[68]

Some white supremacists said that the Keenans' lawsuit, and others like it, improperly manipulate the court system to suppress unpopular political views. The Aryan Nations website said that the Southern Poverty Law Center was a "Marxist anti-Christ anti-White Jewish cabal [plotting group]" that brought about a "contrived trial brought solely for the purpose of bankrupting a small Christian organization."[69]

Those who bring lawsuits such as Victoria Keenan's do not deny that they seek to use the legal system as a weapon against hate groups. As two lawyers for the Southern Poverty Law Center wrote in an article in 1995,

> Our goal in the Portland case [on behalf of the family of Mulugeta Seraw] and similar lawsuits has been to hold the leaders of hate groups responsible for the violent actions of their members. First, we aim to bankrupt the organizations or individuals responsible for hate crimes. Second, we seek to separate the footsoldiers from the leaders, whose combined charisma and intelligence make them less replaceable. Through these means, we hope not only to put the hate groups themselves out of business, but to stop their leaders from encouraging so many youths to perpetrate hate violence.[70]

Not surprisingly, lawyers who take hate groups to court dismiss the notion that the lawsuits are an abuse of the legal system and aim to suppress political views in violation of the First Amendment of the U.S. Constitution. Andrew Roth, a lawyer who sued a group called Hammerskin Nation in California for the 1999 beating and stabbing of an African American man in Riverside, California, told the *Los Angeles Times:* "There are 1st Amendment issues that protect political speech, expressions of ideas and philosophy. But the goal is to make sure they [the constitutional principles] don't protect organizations when they advocate . . . specific courses of violence."[71]

President Lyndon Johnson signs the Civil Rights Act of 1964, which prohibits discrimination in the workplace and in public accommodations, such as restaurants and hotels.

Civil rights laws

In many ways, the manner in which the legal system addresses hate-inspired violence is still a work in progress, as debate continues on hate-crime legislation and on the use of civil lawsuits against hate groups. By comparison, the many laws that apply to nonviolent bigotry in the workplace, marketplace, housing, and similar arenas are well-established features on the nation's legal landscape. The main laws that prohibit discrimination have been in effect for years. Among the most important national, or federal, laws is the Civil Rights Act of 1964. The Civil Rights Act prohibits discrimination in public accommodations such as restaurants and hotels, as well as employment discrimination. Another central law is the Voting Rights Act of 1965, which guarantees citizens the right to vote regardless of race, religion, or national origin. The Fair Housing Act of 1968 covers discrimination in the sale or rental of dwellings.

These antidiscrimination laws and others, also called civil rights laws, are complex. And although they are well established compared with the emerging body of hate-crime laws, the civil rights laws are always evolving as well. Lawyers make new uses of them, judges reinterpret their meaning, and legislators amend them. Complicated though the laws may be, their effects are often simple enough: They require corporations (as well as people) that have been found to discriminate in ways that violate the laws to compensate the people who have been discriminated against. The goal of the laws is to provide remedies for the victims of (for example) workplace or housing discrimination, to punish the company or people who discriminated, and to deter discrimination in the future.

Workplace lawsuits

In recent years, major corporations have paid large sums of money to settle cases brought against them charging racial discrimination in employment. (Frequently, parties to a lawsuit agree to a "settlement," in which the party who is said to have discriminated agrees to pay damages or provide other remedies rather than go forward with a trial.) In 2000, for example, the Coca-Cola Company settled a case for a record-breaking $192.5 million, the largest settlement to date in a U.S. race discrimination suit.

Black employees filed the Coca-Cola lawsuit in April 1999. They claimed that company policies kept black employees at the bottom rungs of the corporate ladder, paying them an average of $26,000 a year less than their white counterparts. The Coke settlement provided $113 million to be shared among two thousand African American employees in the suit. Another $43.5 million was paid to increase the salaries of black employees at Coke to make them comparable to pay received by whites. Coke also provided $36 million to fund programs to monitor its employment practices.

In the settlement, Coca-Cola admitted no wrongdoing, which is typical in such settlements. However, most people agreed that the effects of the settlement spoke louder than the words that Coca-Cola did not utter. The lawsuit did not result in only monetary awards for black employees. Coke also agreed to take specific steps to improve the work environment for African American employees and to change its promotion and compensation policies to ensure that blacks were not disadvantaged. As former editor in chief of the magazine *Emerge* wrote,

> Whether Coke admits it or not, everyone knows they are not forking over almost $193 million out of the goodness of their heart. They realize that had the case proceeded to court, they could have been out of much more than $200 million.
>
> After vehemently denying for months that the case had . . . merit, in the end Coca-Cola officials had to acknowledge the obvious.[72]

Coke officials may or may not have thought that the case against them had merit. They may or may not have thought that if the case went to trial, they could have lost more than $200 million. What the Coca-Cola settlement indicates, however, is that antidiscrimination laws can bring about major

Attorney Cyrus Mehri talks to reporters about the $192.5 million settlement reached between the Coca-Cola Company and two thousand African American employees who filed a race discrimination suit against the company.

changes in the workplace. "This settlement sets a new standard for corporate diversity," a lawyer for the Coke employees said in a press release. "In short, the 'World of Coke' will be going through a 'World of Change.'"[73]

Affirmative action

In addition to monetary awards and the adoption of policies aimed at preventing future discrimination, settlements and court orders that arise out of discrimination lawsuits sometimes include a more controversial element: affirmative action. Affirmative action refers to policies that give an advantage, or preference, to minorities over other (generally, white) people. The preferences might apply to hiring for jobs, workplace promotions, government contracts, school admissions, and more. The idea behind affirmative action is that the roots of racism are so deep that they can be overcome only by using race as a factor that counts in favor of minorities. Although the effects of affirmative action are difficult to measure, one study by a Rutgers University professor found that 5 million minority workers had better jobs in 1995 than they would have had without affirmative action and the antidiscrimination laws.

Often, affirmative action has been a tool of government, in which minority preferences have been enacted into laws and carried out by government agencies. For example, many local governments have used minority preferences to hire more minority-owned companies to perform work such as building public highways. State-run universities have implemented affirmative action policies in their admissions processes to attract more minority students to their schools. Sometimes these preferential policies hold minority students to lower standards of admission than other students.

Affirmative action has attracted serious opposition and resentment among some white people. Recently, courts have cut back on affirmative action in government programs, saying that race-conscious preferences amount to "reverse discrimination" that violates the civil rights of nonminorities. Some African Americans also object to affirmative action on the grounds that it taints their actual achievements. Their argument is that, as long as affirmative action exists, people will believe that African Americans in positions of power, influence, or achievement got there not entirely on their own merits but with the extra boost of a minority preference tucked away in a court decree, settlement, or law.

Despite the controversy about race-based preferences, many private businesses find them useful. In particular, leaders of large companies that sell products to a large and diverse marketplace often believe that employment diversity is good business, and that to reach out to potential minority employees, they still need to take affirmative action. In addition, companies such as Texaco, which has been accused of discrimination in the past, may turn to affirmative action policies to fend off future problems.

Texaco's example

Business analysts and others often mention Texaco's affirmative action programs as examples of race-based preferences that have helped a company change for the better. In 1996, Texaco paid $176.1 million to end a discrimination lawsuit brought by African American employees. The employees claimed that they were paid less than their job category required because they were minorities. But the bigotry problem at Texaco was not limited to disparities in pay and job opportunities. In November 1996 the *New York Times* printed a front-page story based on secret tape recordings a former top Texaco official had made of meetings of him and other officials discussing the lawsuit. They used racial epithets and talked of destroying evidence. Separately, Bari-Ellen Roberts, a black former senior financial analyst at Texaco who had been one of the plaintiffs, later published a book with details about humiliations she and other black employees had suffered. She wrote about the time her performance review was downgraded because a white supervisor found her "uppity" and another time when a white official referred to her publicly as a "little colored girl."[74]

After the settlement, the company's chief executive officer, Peter I. Bijur, conducted an investigation. Upon finding that the largely white, male company had fostered an atmosphere of bigotry, he set out to increase Texaco's diversity. His efforts

included hiring search firms known to have proven records of recruiting minority workers and setting up scholarship and internship programs to attract minorities to engineering, physical sciences, information systems, and international business. He told senior executives that their career advancements would be directly linked to their success in implementing the new diversity initiatives. He hired African American executives for top positions. The company also vowed to spend at least $1 billion with minority- and women-owned vendors—about 15 percent of overall spending—before 2001.

Sil Chambers and Bari-Ellen Roberts, two plaintiffs in the discrimination suit against Texaco, hold a press conference after the company agreed to pay $176.1 million to settle the case.

The results were promising. In 1998, minorities accounted for nearly four in ten new hires at Texaco, and more than 20 percent of promotions. During the first six months of 1999, minorities made up 44 percent of new hires and 22 percent of promotions. Even Bari-Ellen Roberts, the former employee whose book exposed blatant racism at Texaco, conceded in a 1999 interview, "They've made progress. They had to—things could not stay the same."[75]

Of the efforts to change Texaco, chief executive officer Bijur told *Business Week* magazine in 2000: "It's never over."[76] Whether affirmative action itself is also "never over" in a company's efforts to build a prejudice-free and successful workplace is another, more difficult question. Some white people who lose out on jobs or promotions in the workplace—or on admissions to universities or on contracts to build highways—believe that they should not be discriminated against to make up for discrimination that they did not engage in years before. Ironically, affirmative action programs, designed to fight bigotry, may sometimes have the effect of creating bigotry, for some whites come to resent the minorities who are helped by these programs.

Freedom to insult

Discrimination in the workplace is a serious and widespread problem, but bigoted speech—from insults directed at an individual because of his or her religion to racial slurs that generalize about all members of a group—is probably the type of bigotry that people encounter most in their day-to-day lives. Although such bigotry can sometimes be addressed through legal tools, the law is limited in this regard. This is because the First Amendment to the U.S. Constitution protects a person's ability to say what he or she wants free from interference or censorship by the government, including the courts. In many—but not all—circumstances, bigoted speech is shielded from legal consequences because of this constitutional principle.

First Amendment protection for individual expression is strongest when that speech is uttered in public places, such as streets and parks, particularly in the forms of protests and demonstrations. Judges have preserved the right of neo-Nazis to hold marches and rallies, even in communities with large Jewish populations who object to the Nazi presence. The U.S. Supreme Court ruled that a St. Paul, Minnesota, city ordinance banning cross burnings because of their racist and anti-Semitic messages violated the First Amendment and could not be enforced. (For First Amendment purposes, courts have long ruled that "speech" includes actions that are

meant to convey ideas, such as cross burnings or demonstrations.) These rulings do not reflect sympathy or favor for the bigoted messages. They reflect the value that the U.S. Constitution and the American legal system place on unfettered expression as a central tenet of American life and as the best means to preserve individual freedom.

The U.S. Supreme Court has ruled that cross burnings are protected by the First Amendment, and therefore cannot be banned.

But not all hate speech is protected. The Supreme Court has said that speech that advocates violence and that is likely immediately to produce unlawful violence is not protected by the First Amendment. Similarly, a threat to harm another person, if specific and credible, is not protected speech.

In addition, the legal concepts of libel and slander can act as a brake on a person's right to spew hate speech. Libel is a claim in which one individual alleges that another's written words have damaged his or her reputation; slander is a similar legal claim involving spoken words. In general, a person may sue another for libel or slander (and receive monetary damages) if the speech in question was both false and defamatory. Something is defamatory if it tends to hold a person up to ridicule, contempt, shame, or disgrace. So if a bigoted person writes an article in which he or she falsely says that a particular black man was a rapist or that a Jewish person engaged in dishonest business practices, the writer may be subject to a lawsuit for libel.

Finally, although the First Amendment forbids the government from restricting speech, it does not apply to private parties. Employers, organizations, and individuals are entitled to prohibit racist and bigoted expression or behavior on their property. The same neo-Nazi who is free to demonstrate with a swastika and a banner decrying Jews in a town square is not free to spray paint a swastika on a synagogue. That type of speech is punishable by criminal and civil laws that bar, for example, trespassing and harassment.

Bigotry.com

In recent years, the Internet has become the town square where hate groups and bigoted individuals disseminate their messages. Here, too, the First Amendment shields most racist, anti-Semitic, and other bigoted speech. Websites and e-mails that threaten violence against specific individuals are not protected (just as specific threats are not protected in the "real" world), but it is easier for people who make such threats to hide their identities on the Internet than elsewhere.

Despite the speech protections of the First Amendment and the difficulties in tracking down e-mail correspondents, the legal system has shut down at least some Internet bigots. In 1998, for example, a former University of California student was sentenced to one year in prison for sending e-mail death threats to sixty Asian American students. His messages said that he hated Asians and blamed them for problems at the school. The messages said he would "make it my life career to find and kill everyone [*sic*] . . . of you personally."[77]

In another case, a college student pleaded guilty to federal civil rights charges in February 1999 after sending hate-filled e-mails to Latinos across the country. He received a two-year

Abraham Foxman, national director of the Anti-Defamation League, shows hate material from an Internet site. The Internet has become an anonymous, efficient method for hate groups to disseminate their messages.

sentence for sending the derogatory messages, which said that Latinos were too stupid to get jobs or go to college without the help of affirmative action programs. The messages also threatened to kill the recipients.

The limits of the law

Criminal prosecutions and civil lawsuits are useful in fighting bigotry. As Martin Luther King Jr. said, "Morality cannot be legislated, but behavior can be regulated. Judicial decrees may not change the heart, but they can restrain the heartless."[78] Still, lawsuits and judicial decrees are limited. Everyday bigoted speech is mostly beyond the reach of legal tools. Affirmative action as a means of remedying discrimination has created a white backlash and has been found by many judges and legal experts to pose legal problems of its own. Civil rights lawsuits can bring tangible rewards to victims of bigotry in the workplace and other settings, and can even lead some people and corporations to change their behavior. But the lawsuits are complex and expensive.

As for hate groups, a combination of criminal and civil cases can sometimes put a dent in their ability to pursue their goals, but hate groups are resilient. In 2001, when legal proceedings deprived Richard Butler's Aryan Nations of its twenty-acre rural compound as a gathering and training place for white supremacists, the group's followers immediately started planning their annual meeting at a different locale. Some also started reorganizing under the banner of a different group, also promoted by Butler.

Legal institutions and processes surely have a role in fighting bigotry—mainly the role of compensating those who are wronged by illegal bigoted action and holding responsible those who perform the wrongs. But neither laws nor lawsuits nor court orders necessarily "change the heart" of bigotry, in the words of Martin Luther King Jr. And changing hearts is what it will take for society to overcome bigotry and prejudice in the most meaningful and lasting way.

6

Changing the Heart of Bigotry

RULES AND LAWS can scratch only the surface of bigotry in the United States today, so many people have taken up other methods to chip away at prejudice and try to build a more tolerant society. Individuals, as well as schools, communities, businesses, and organizations, fight bigotry through education, information, counseling, and social opportunities. Success in these efforts is rarely seen overnight. Indeed, success is sometimes not seen at all. This is not surprising, given the deep roots of prejudice and continuing conditions that feed into stereotypes and bigotry. As Gordon Alport, a leading investigator into the causes and nature of prejudice, wrote in *The Nature of Prejudice,* "It required years of labor and billions of dollars to gain the secret of the atom. It will take a still greater investment to gain the secrets of man's irrational nature. It is easier, someone has said, to smash an atom than a prejudice."[79]

Despite the difficulties, for many people, fighting bigotry is as important a task in modern society as fighting disease. After all, the victims of bigotry represent a wide variety of Americans, great in both numbers and diversity. Those who work to eliminate bigotry believe that society is deprived when these people are not permitted to live as fully and freely as the population at large, and thus do not contribute as fully to the nation's economic, political, and cultural fabric. In addition, to the extent that bigotry causes instability and violence in American communities, the reduction of bigotry may translate into a more peaceful society.

Diversity training

The leaders of many large corporations and businesses have come to view both blatant and subtle bias as bad for the bottom line. In their view, bias and bigotry can upset employees (reducing productivity), lead to legal problems, and deprive companies of the talents of minority workers. In recent years, therefore, many businesses have worked to root out bigotry on the job. Some companies hire experts to help them address the problem of prejudice. Often, a key component of the solution is *diversity training*, which is aimed at teaching people to recognize their prejudices toward others, to understand the harm prejudice causes, and to eliminate or control bias.

For example, after Denny's restaurants faced three race discrimination lawsuits in the early 1990s, its leaders went to

As a result of changes implemented by the company after discrimination lawsuits in the early 1990s, Denny's restaurants are now considered by experts to be among the best places for minorities and women to work.

Mr. Ron Petty

great efforts to change the corporate culture. They wanted to create a workplace where African Americans would be welcomed to work, and a restaurant chain that treated all customers with the same respect. When Jim Adamson became the chief executive officer of Denny's parent corporation, called Flagstar, in 1995, he immediately implemented changes to increase diversity.

Among the changes he introduced were training programs to give African Americans and other minorities opportunities to rise to executive ranks in the company. Adamson also implemented a fast-track program to encourage minorities to own individual Denny's restaurants. He introduced new interviewing techniques to identify job applicants with bigoted attitudes. Finally, Denny's employees were required to attend diversity training that showed them how to treat customers equally. Employees watched videotapes on the wrong and right way to serve customers. About the diversity training, Rachelle Hood-Phillips, a top Flagstar executive, told *Fortune* magazine, "We want to help people communicate and connect across a line of difference. We want to change their hearts, their perspectives, and their behavior." [80]

The efforts have reduced bigotry at Denny's. The restaurant that a decade ago achieved notoriety for its refusal to serve African Americans now is often named by experts as among the best places for minorities and women to work. But, according to CEO Jim Adamson, the success is incomplete. Because of bigotry, the chain lost customers who have not come back. Adamson says, "The biggest costs [of Denny's past prejudice] are people, [who] because of our history, have elected to eat elsewhere. . . . It is really sad when you're in the service business and people perceive that you don't value them." [81]

Changing perceptions

Changing people's perceptions is central to fighting bigotry. While business leaders such as Jim Adamson struggle to change perceptions that their corporations are bigoted, other leaders struggle to change perceptions about minorities that people rely on to justify their bigotry. They want to teach

Judy and Dennis Shepard, the parents of Matthew Shepard, speak at the Democratic National Convention. Since her son's death, Judy has become committed to changing negative attitudes toward homosexuals.

children, parents, teachers, and others that stereotypes are often wrong and harmful. These people believe that, just as bigoted thinking can be learned, tolerance can be learned as well.

For example, the mother of Matthew Shepard, the young man who was brutally murdered outside Laramie, Wyoming, in 1999 because he was gay, gives speeches, makes public service announcements for television, and has participated in a documentary film. Her goal is to humanize gay people and change attitudes toward them, particularly the attitudes of students and school administrators. One of the public service announcements she made, which aired on MTV in 1999 (reaching 30 to 45 million young viewers), showed students shouting "homo," "faggot," and "queer." In between these images were pictures of Matthew Shepard and the words "murdered/because he was gay/end/hate." Judy Shepard's voice is then heard: "The next time you use words like these, think about what they really mean."[82]

MTV launched other efforts to show young viewers the consequences of bigotry. Beginning at 10 P.M. on January 10,

2001, the network aired no programs and no commercials for eighteen consecutive hours. Instead, viewers saw a black screen that posted the names and stories of hundreds of hate-crime victims. MTV is the same network that in the past had promoted rapper Eminem, famous for his violent antigay lyrics.

Part of MTV's antibigotry campaign was a new Internet forum on discrimination as part of its website, *MTV.com*. The effort showed just how difficult fighting bigotry can be. Although the forum was established to foster discussion about fighting hate, many people used it for another purpose: to promote hate. "The haters came out of the woodwork," Nicholas Butterworth, an MTV official, told the *Washington Post*. "A frightening amount [of messages] have been hateful, homophobic, and racist." Although this was not the response MTV had hoped for, Butterworth said that *MTV.com* would not remove all the hateful posts so that viewers might learn something from reading bigotry in the raw: "We don't want to delete everything. One of the reasons for the epidemic of hate-related crimes is because there isn't enough awareness of diversity. . . . The best way to deal with hateful attitudes is to expose them so people can see how strong and violent they are."[83]

Face-to-face

Sometimes, face-to-face interaction among people of different races, nationalities, or religions is the most direct and effective way to shatter stereotypes and break bigotry. The world of youth and school sports, in particular, creates opportunities for individuals to build relationships with people of different races and ethnicities. These relationships enable the participants to see beyond their differences and value the contributions of people who are different from themselves.

A clear example of this was depicted in the 2000 movie *Remember the Titans*, starring Denzel Washington. *Titans* was based on the Alexandria, Virginia, high school football team, the T. C. Williams Titans, which struggled to overcome racial divisiveness and build a cohesive and winning team of black and white players during the 1971 season. At the time, the school was a newly merged agglomeration of three different high schools. State officials had combined them into one school in the hopes that it would bring greater unity to the Alexandria community, which had been troubled by racial tensions.

In hiring a head football coach for the new school, officials passed over a popular white former head coach in favor of defensive backfield coach Herman Boone. Boone was African American. In a 2000 interview, Boone explained that being on a team together fostered communication among different students, which in turn reduced bigotry. He said,

> [Reducing bigotry is] about communication. Talking to each other. We forced the kids to spend time with each other, find out things about each other. Every player was required to spend time with teammates that were a different race. And you know, once they started doing that, they discovered they liked their teammates. That was the turning point. [84]

Coach Herman Boone with players on the 1971 T. C. Williams High School football team. The team's experiences overcoming bigotry were depicted in the 2000 film, Remember the Titans.

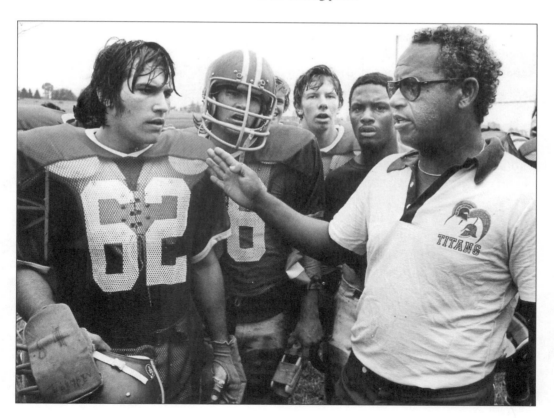

A reporter who covered high school football and the Titans in 1971 also observed the bigotry-busting power of student athletics. He wrote,

> As the team grew closer, the school did as well. Two players in particular . . . became ambassadors on the field. When they first met, they intensely disliked each other. But by the time the season was halfway over, they were close friends. . . .
>
> When the cliques from each of the three schools saw the players getting along, they started to dissolve. After a couple of weeks, there was only one pep club, and the rest of the school started a slow, but steady, "us" attitude instead of them. [85]

The T. C. Williams Titans got to the state championship with a record of twelve wins and no losses. The team's victory at state was 27–0.

The Titans' experience illustrates the power of sports—in which team members must cooperate, depend on each other's strengths, and accept each other's differences—as an antidote to bigotry. But youth sports are not a perfect solution. Patrick Welsh, an English teacher at T. C. Williams who was in his second year of teaching during that 1971 season, agrees that sports can create powerful bonds between students of different races and shatter stereotypes. But, he wrote in 2000,

> Today, at T. C. Williams and, I suspect, at many other schools, too many kids are being deprived of that Titans-like bonding experience because sports themselves have become stereotyped. There are "black" sports and "white" sports, and few students dare to cross the racial divide. [86]

Still, students who do venture across the color line are likely to experience breakthroughs in understanding bigotry. In his 2000 article, Welsh quoted Liz Johnson, a white athlete, who starred at T. C. Williams five years earlier in two "white sports," field hockey and soccer. Johnson said that her greatest experience was in basketball, a "black girl" sport:

> It was the first time I had to work to be accepted, but once I was, there was a natural growth of friendship, not some phony "I'm going to find a black friend" thing. . . . I was exposed to the covert racism the black players always faced. When we went to play white schools, everyone was afraid of us because we had

so many blacks on the team. It was the "I'm not a racist, it's just that these girls are dangerous" kind of attitude.[87]

A chain of change

As Liz Johnson's experience suggests, the prevention or elimination of bigotry happens one person at a time—perhaps through a white girl joining a mostly black basketball team or a restaurant employee working to improve service to all customers. Sometimes an entire community can be affected as an antibigotry message makes its way from person to person. This is what happened in Billings, Montana. There, in the weeks before Christmas in 1993, white supremacists went on a rampage. They vandalized Jewish graves. They spray painted the home of a Native American with racist graffiti. They went to an African American church during religious services and hovered threateningly in the back.

Then a chunk of cinder block was thrown through the upstairs window of six-year-old Isaac Schnitzer's bedroom. In the window had been a Hanukkah menorah. Police who responded to the incident advised Isaac's mother to remove all Jewish symbols from their home. But she refused, and her neighbors found out. They held vigils, signed petitions, and repainted houses defaced by racist graffiti. Soon the town was awash in menorahs—real ones, which people bought, and pictures of menorahs cut out of the *Billings Gazette*. The bigots responded by throwing rocks and shooting out windows, but the menorahs remained. When Isaac saw the menorahs around town, he asked his mother, "Are they Jewish, too?"

"No," she answered him, "they're friends."[88]

By the end of December, ten thousand people in Billings displayed menorahs in their windows. The manager of a local sporting goods store put on his street sign, in foot-high letters, "Not in Our Town. No Hate. No Violence. Peace on Earth."[89] The sign and slogan received attention across the United States, with a television special, a Hollywood movie, and a tolerance movement taking up the cry.

The nation's population is becoming increasingly diverse. It is up to each individual to decide whether he or she will embrace this diversity or cling to views that perpetuate prejudice and intolerance of other groups.

No one expects bigotry simply to disappear as a result of these and other efforts. Sometimes efforts to reduce bigotry backfire, and interactions between different groups can create more, instead of less, suspicion. During the next several decades, opportunities for more interactions among different racial, national, and ethnic groups in the United States will multiply as the nation's population becomes ever more diverse. According to estimates, by 2010, Latinos will replace African Americans as the largest minority group in the United States. By 2020 the number of people with Asian backgrounds will double, from around 10 million to 20 million. By 2050 whites will still be the majority racial group, but just barely—and after 2053, whites are expected to make up less than half of the U.S. population.

What these numbers mean is that, in the years ahead, stereotypes and bigotry will have many opportunities to weaken—and just as many chances to get stronger. The direction in which society moves concerning bigotry depends on many factors, from economic conditions to psychological issues that scientists do not even fully understand. None of these factors, however, is necessarily more important than the everyday actions of mere individuals, who may respond to the complexities of a diverse world by embracing simplistic, bigoted conclusions or by embracing diversity itself.

Notes

Introduction

1. Quoted in Jeff Pearlman, "At Full Blast," *Sports Illustrated Online*, December 23, 1999. sportsillustrated.cnn.com/features/cover/news/1999/12/22/rocker.

2. Quoted in Pearlman, "At Full Blast."

3. Quoted in David Segal, "Grammys' Discordant Note," *Washington Post*, January 5, 2001, pp. A1, A12.

4. Quoted in Segal, "Grammys' Discordant Note," p. A12.

5. Quoted in Anti-Defamation League, "Close the Book on Hate." www.adl.org/ctboh/kids_do.html.

Chapter 1: The Many Faces of Bigotry

6. Quoted in Annie Murphy Paul, "Where Bias Begins: The Truth About Stereotypes," *Psychology Today*, June 1998, p. 52.

7. Quoted in Howard Chua-Eoan, "Profiles in Outrage: America Is Home, but Asian Americans Sometimes Feel Treated as Outlanders with Unproven Loyalties," *Time*, September 25, 2000, pp. 40, 42.

8. Wilhelmina A. Leigh, "Institutional Racism, Part III: Racism or Preference? The Role of 'Soft Skills' in Hiring," *Nation's Cities Weekly*, June 26, 2000, p. 4.

9. David Pilgrim, "The Brute Caricature," Jim Crow Museum of Racist Memorabilia, November 2000. www.ferris.edu/news/jimcrow.

10. Quoted in Pilgrim, "The Brute Caricature."

11. Quoted in Vern E. Smith and Andrew Murr, "Up from Jim Crow," *Newsweek*, September 18, 2000, pp. 42, 44.

12. Lyndon Baines Johnson, "Special Message to the Congress: The American Promise," Lyndon Baines Johnson Library and Museum home page, March 15, 1965. www.lbjlib. utexas.edu/johnson/archives.hom/speeches.hom/special_ messages.asp.

13. Quoted in Ilene Cooper, "To Bigotry No Sanction: The Story of the Oldest Synagogue in America" [book review], *Booklist*, February 1, 1999, p. 971.

14. Quoted in Anti-Defamation League, "The International Jew: Anti-Semitism from the Roaring Twenties Revived on the Web," July 1999. www.adl.org/special_reports/ij/intro.html.

15. Quoted in Anti-Defamation League, "Poisoning the Web: Holocaust Denial," 2000. www.adl.org/poisoning_web/holocaust _denial.html.

16. Dale Russakoff, "Expressions of Pride, Worries of Prejudice," *Washington Post*, August 8, 2000, p. A12.

Chapter 2: The Causes of Bigotry

17. "Race and Recognition," *Washington Post*, December 4, 2000, p. A11.

18. Quoted in Anti-Defamation League, "Close the Book on Hate."

19. Public Broadcasting System, "Clinton Sipes' Story," *Not in Our Town*. www.pbs.org/niot/programs/clinton.htm.

20. Quoted in Dave Cullen, "The Reluctant Activist," *Salon News*, October 15, 1999. www.salon.com/news/feature/1999/ 10/15/laramie.

21. Quoted in Patrick Welsh, "At T. C. Williams, Separate Fields of Play," *Washington Post*, October 22, 2000, pp. B1, B4.

22. Thomas Sowell, "Lucrative Bigotry," *Forbes*, May 9, 1994, p. 117.

23. Quoted in Richard D. Kahlenberg, *Race* [book review], *Washington Post*, February 4, 2001, p. 4.

24. Quoted in Kahlenberg, *Race*, p. 4.

25. Chris Tilly, "Institutional Racism, Part II: Race, Skill, and Hiring in U.S. Cities," *Nation's Cities Weekly*, June 19, 2000, p. 4.

26. Quoted in Lynette Clemetson, "Trying to Right Mr. Wong: The Web Site's Founders Say It's Entertainment. But Asian-Americans Say It's Offensive—and Dangerous," *Newsweek,* July 31, 2000, p. 55.

27. Quoted in Paul Farhi, "Reality TV Broadcasts 'Bad Black Guy' Stereotype," *Washington Post*, February 20, 2001, p. C1.

28. Quoted in Farhi, "Reality TV," *Washington Post*, p. C1.

29. Quoted in Jack E. White, "Imus 'n' Andy: The Radio Host and His Sidekicks Trade in Bigotry," *Time*, May 22, 2000, p. 49.

30. "Closet Racism," *Broadcasting and Cable*, September 11, 2000, p. 4.

Chapter 3: Living with Bigotry

31. Quoted in Roger Campbell, "Living While Black," *Essence*, November 2000, p. 90.

32. Campbell, "Living While Black," p. 90.

33. Quoted in Faye Rice, "Denny's Changes Its Spots," *Fortune*, May 12, 1996. www.fortune.com/fortune/magazine/1996/960513/managing3.html.

34. Quoted in Rice, "Denny's Changes Its Spots."

35. Quoted in Sheila Kaplan, "The New Face of Racism," *U.S. News & World Report*, January 3, 2000. www.usnews.com/usnews/issue/000103/race.htm.

36. Quoted in Kaplan, "The New Face of Racism."

37. Quoted in Kaplan, "The New Face of Racism."

38. John Derbyshire, "In Defense of Racial Profiling," *National Review*, February 19, 2001, pp. 38, 39. www.nationalreview.com/19feb01/derbyshire021901.shtml.

39. Derbyshire, "In Defense of Racial Profiling," p. 39.

40. Quoted in Kaplan, "The New Face of Racism."

41. John Bentacur, "Institutional Racism, Part I: The Impacts on Access to Education and Employment," *Nation's Cities Weekly*, June 12, 2000, p. 1.

42. Bentacur, "Institutional Racism, Part I."

43. Tilly, "Institutional Racism, Part II."

44. Tilly, "Institutional Racism, Part II."

45. Quoted in Gregory D. Squires, "The Indelible Color Line," *American Prospect*, January 1999. www.prospect.org/authors/squires-g.html.

46. Rebecca Gordon, Libero Della Piana, and Terry Keleher, *Facing the Consequences: An Examination of Racial Discrimination in U.S. Public Schools*. Oakland, CA: Applied Research Center, 2000, p. 1.

47. Gordon, Della Piana, and Keleher, *Facing the Consequences*, pp. 8–9.

48. Gordon, Della Piana, and Keleher, *Facing the Consequences*, p. 12.

49. Quoted in Jay Mathews, "Study Finds Racial Bias in Special Ed," *Washington Post*, March 3, 2001, p. A1.

50. Quoted in Mathews, "Study Finds Racial Bias in Special Ed," p. A10.

51. Quoted in Sharon Begley, "The Stereotype Trap," *Newsweek*, November 6, 2000, p. 66.

Chapter 4: Extremes of Bigotry: Hate Groups and Hate Crimes

52. National Alliance, "What Is the National Alliance? National Alliance Goals." www.natvan.com.

53. National Alliance, "What Is the National Alliance?"

54. Anti-Defamation League, "Explosion of Hate: The Growing Danger of the National Alliance," 2000. www.adl.org/explosion_of_hate/explosion_of_hate.html.

55. National Alliance, "Who Rules America?" June 2000. www.natvan.com/who-rules-america.

56. World Church of the Creator, "Frequently Asked Questions About Creativity." www.creator.org/faq.html.

57. World Church of the Creator, "Frequently Asked Questions."

58. Quoted in James Willwerth, "Confessions of a Skinhead," *Time*, August 19, 1996. www.time.com/time/magazine/archive/1996/dom/960819/skins.html.

59. Quoted in Willwerth, "Confessions of a Skinhead."

60. Quoted in Dennis McCafferty, "Desperately Seeking Angry White Females," *Salon News*, October 14, 1999. www.salon.com/news/feature/1999/10/14/hate/index.html.

61. Quoted in McCafferty, "Desperately Seeking Angry White Females."

62. Kim Murphy, "Lawsuits Threaten to Drain the Life out of Hate Groups," *Los Angeles Times*, August 22, 2000. www.latimes.com.

63. Quoted in Anti-Defamation League, "Resistance Records a Cash Cow for Hate Movement" [press release], June 5, 2000. www.adl.org/PresRele/Asus_12/3620_12.html.

64. Southern Poverty Law Center, *Ten Ways to Fight Hate*. Montgomery, AL: Southern Poverty Law Center, 1999, p. 10.

65. Quoted in "Cuomo Says Million Dollar Award Sends Clear Message Against Racial Discrimination on the Internet," HUD Press Release No. 00-165, July 20, 2000. www.hud.gov/pressrel/pr00-165.html.

66. Quoted in "Cuomo Says Million Dollar Award Sends Clear Message Against Racial Discrimination on the Internet."

67. Southern Poverty Law Center, *Ten Ways to Fight Hate*, p. 10.

Chapter 5: The Law and Bigotry

68. Quoted in David Neiwert, "Hate Group Loses Property to Two Who Won Lawsuit," *Washington Post*, February 14, 2001, p. A3.

69. Quoted in William Claiborne, "Supremacy Group Faces Fateful Trial," *Washington Post*, August 28, 2000, p. A3.

70. Morris Dees and Ellen Bowden, "Taking Hate Groups to Court," February 1995. www.splcenter.org.

71. Quoted in Murphy, "Lawsuits Threaten to Drain the Life Out of Hate Groups."

72. George E. Curry, "Racism Costs Corporate America," *New Journal & Guide*, December 7, 2000. www.njournalg.com/editorial/2000/12/curr_racism_costs.html.

73. Quoted in "Coke to Settle Race Bias Case for $192.5 Million," *Muzi.com News*, November 17, 2000. www.dailynews.muzi.com.

74. Quoted in Kenneth Labich, "No More Crude at Texaco," *Fortune*, September 6, 1999, pp. 205, 208.

75. Quoted in Labich, "No More Crude at Texaco," p. 210.

76. Quoted in "Rooting Out Racism," *Business Week*, January 10, 2000, p. 66.

77. Quoted in Anti-Defamation League, "Responding to Extremist Speech Online: 10 Frequently Asked Questions," Question 3. www.adl.org/issue_combating_hate/10faq.

78. Quoted in Anti-Defamation League, "Counteracting Hate Crimes: A National Priority," October 1997. www.adl.org/opinion/counter_hatecrimes.html.

Chapter 6: Changing the Heart of Bigotry

79. Quoted in Sherry Godfrey, Charles L. Richman, and Taryn N. Withers, "Reliability and Validity of a New Scale to Measure Prejudice: The GRISMS," *Current Psychology*, Spring 2000, p. 3.

80. Quoted in Rice, "Denny's Changes Its Spots."

81. Quoted in "Coke Settles Discrimination Suit," *About.com*, December 2000. racerelations.about.com/newsissues/racerelations/library/weekly/aa112000a.htm.

82. Quoted in Cullen, "The Reluctant Activist."

83. Quoted in Kimberly Shearer Palmer, "MTV: Battling Hate Online," *Washington Post*, February 1, 2001, p. C4.

84. Quoted in Don Bowman, "Remembering the Titans: In 1971, an Integrated High School Football Team Won More Than the Virginia State Title; It Also Beat Racism," *Knight-Ridder/Tribune News Service*, October 19, 2000. www.star-telegram.com.

85. Bowman, "Remembering the Titans."

86. Welsh, "At T. C. Williams, Separate Fields of Play," p. B4.

87. Quoted in Welsh, "At T. C. Williams, Separate Fields of Play," p. B4.

88. Quoted in Southern Poverty Law Center, *Ten Ways to Fight Hate*, p. 9.

89. Quoted in Southern Poverty Law Center, *Ten Ways to Fight Hate*, p. 9.

Organizations to Contact

The following organizations are concerned with bigotry and prejudice. The issues they address include discrimination, hate crimes, and programs to fight bigotry.

American-Arab Anti-Discrimination Committee
4201 Connecticut Ave., NW, Suite 300
Washington, DC 20008
(202) 244-2990
website: www.adc.org

Founded in 1980 by a former U.S. senator, this organization is concerned with discrimination against people of Arab descent. The committee fights negative stereotypes about Arabs through education, advocacy, legal proceedings, and cultural events.

Anti-Defamation League
823 United Nations Plaza
New York, NY 10017
(212) 885-7700
website: www.adl.org

The Anti-Defamation League fights bigotry in general and anti-Semitism in particular. It serves as a public resource for information about a broad range of bigotry-related issues. It also monitors bigotry in everyday life as well as extremist groups.

Asian American Legal Defense and Education Fund (AALDEF)
99 Hudson St., 12th Floor
New York, NY 10013
(212) 966-5932
website: www.aaldef.org

The AALDEF was founded in 1974 by a group of lawyers, law students, and community activists concerned about social and economic justice for Asian Americans. The organization works to combat hate violence against Asian Americans, to remove barriers to the right to vote, and to preserve affirmative action for minorities. The AALDEF also has led efforts to gain redress for Japanese Americans who were unjustly imprisoned in U.S. internment camps during World War II.

Facing History and Ourselves
16 Hurd Rd.
Brookline, MA 02445
(617) 232-1595
website: www.facing.org

Using lessons from history, Facing History and Ourselves aims to teach young people how to be responsible citizens and to preserve freedom. Through its programs, students, teachers, and others learn about racism, prejudice, and anti-Semitism. The organization provides schools with materials and speakers, and helps teachers design lessons that relate history to current problems.

Gay, Lesbian, and Straight Education Network (GLSEN)
121 West 27th St.
New York, NY 10001
(212) 727-0135
www.glsen.org

GLSEN is a leading resource and voice against antigay bias. It fights discrimination against gay people in schools, including students. GLSEN also engages in educational activities to promote tolerance and discourage harassment of gay students and teachers.

Leadership Conference on Civil Rights
1629 K St., NW, Suite 1010
Washington, DC 20006
(202) 466-3311
website: www.civilrights.org

The Leadership Conference on Civil Rights has been involved in antidiscrimination activities for some fifty years. It consists of more than 185 national organizations, which represent a wide range of Americans, including African Americans, gay people, women, religious groups, and more.

National Association for the Advancement of Colored People (NAACP)
4805 Mt. Hope Dr.
Baltimore, MD 21215
(410) 358-8900
website: www.naacp.org

Founded in 1909 in response to the lynchings of African Americans, the NAACP says it is the nation's largest civil rights organization. Since its beginnings, the NAACP has been involved in the major battles against racism in the United States, from school desegregation to fair housing, voting rights, employment discrimination, and more.

National Congress of American Indians
1301 Connecticut Ave., NW, Suite 200
Washington, DC 20036
(202) 466-7767
website: www.ncai.org

This organization was founded in 1944 to safeguard the rights of Native Americans. It engages in advocacy and public information on issues of importance to Native Americans.

National Council of La Raza
1111 19th St., NW, Suite 1000
Washington, DC 20036
(202) 785-1670
website: www.nclr.org

Created in 1968, this group works to reduce discrimination and poverty among Hispanic Americans. La Raza says it is the largest national Hispanic organization in the United States, and it serves people of all Hispanic nationality groups.

Simon Wiesenthal Center
1399 South Roxbury
Los Angeles, CA 90035
(310) 553-9036 or (800) 900-9036
website: www.wiesenthal.org

The Simon Wiensenthal Center is a major resource for information about the Holocaust and anti-Semitism. Its goal is to preserve the memory of the Holocaust by promoting tolerance and action against racism and anti-Semitism. The center runs the Museum of Tolerance in Los Angeles, a hands-on museum that focuses on bigotry in the United States and the history of the Holocaust.

Southern Poverty Law Center

400 Washington Ave.
Montgomery, AL 36104
(334) 264-0286
website: www.splcenter.org

The Southern Poverty Law Center fights hatred, intolerance, and discrimination through education programs and legal action. It publishes *Teaching Tolerance* magazine as well as other educational resources.

Suggestions for Further Reading

Jules Archer, *They Had a Dream*. New York: Viking, 1993. This volume contains biographies of four people who were central figures in black Americans' struggle against discrimination in the United States: Frederick Douglass, Marcus Garvey, Martin Luther King Jr., and Malcolm X.

Robert Baird and Stuart E. Rosenbaum, eds., *Hatred, Bigotry, and Prejudice*. Amherst, NY: Prometheus Books, 1999. This is a collection of writings on bigotry, ranging from historical essays to articles by modern commentators.

Ed Clayton, *Martin Luther King: The Peaceful Warrior*. New York: Pocket Books, 1969. This biography of Dr. King takes the reader from his childhood through his leadership of the civil rights movement in the 1950s and 1960s, which ended with his assassination in 1968.

Kathlyn Gay, *Neo-Nazis: A Growing Threat*. Springfield, NJ: Enslow, 1997. This book examines the origins and activities of neo-Nazi and white supremacist groups. The scope of the white supremacy movement, its goals, and victims are covered, as are ways in which individuals and organizations combat hatred and violence against nonwhites, Jews, and other minorities.

Patricia and Frederick McKissack, *The Civil Rights Movement in America*. Chicago: Children's Press, 1991. This history of the fight against discrimination and racism in America starts in 1865, after the Civil War, and runs through the early 1990s. It includes accounts of the events and people involved as well as illustrations.

Charles Patterson, *Anti-Semitism: The Road to the Holocaust and Beyond.* New York: Walker, 1982. This book examines the history of prejudice against Jews from ancient times to the end of the twentieth century.

Mary Williams, ed., *Discrimination: Opposing Viewpoints.* San Diego: Greenhaven Press, 1997. In this collection of essays and articles, opposing arguments are presented on a wide variety of topics relating to discrimination.

————, *Issues in Racism.* San Diego: Lucent Books, 2000. The author examines current controversies about race in America, including affirmative action, racial profiling, and hate crimes.

Works Consulted

Books

Jim Carnes, ed., *Responding to Hate at School.* Montgomery, AL: Southern Poverty Law Center, 1999. A handbook to help school communities identify, respond to, and discourage bigotry at school.

Rebecca Gordon, Libero Della Piana, and Terry Keleher, *Facing the Consequences: An Examination of Racial Discrimination in U.S. Public Schools.* Oakland, CA: Applied Research Center, 2000. Researchers argue that students of color receive a second-rate education in America's public schools.

Southern Poverty Law Center, *Ten Ways to Fight Hate.* Montgomery, AL: Southern Poverty Law Center, 1999. Published by a leading antibigotry group, this book includes details of how individuals and communities have fought hate crimes.

Periodicals

Bill Archer, "Texas Health Exec Quits After Making Racial Slurs," *Jet*, November 13, 2000.

Sharon Begley, "The Stereotype Trap," *Newsweek*, November 6, 2000.

John Bentacur, "Institutional Racism, Part I: The Impacts on Access to Education and Employment," *Nation's Cities Weekly,* June 12, 2000.

William Booth, "California's Ethnic Diversity Grows," *Washington Post*, March 30, 2001.

Angela Bouwsma, "Showing His True Colors," *Newsweek*, February 24, 1997.

Donna Britt, "It's Too Soon to Say We Knew Ashcroft's Heart," *Washington Post*, January 12, 2001.

Roger Campbell, "Living While Black," *Essence*, November 2000.

Howard Chua-Eoan, "Profiles in Outrage: America Is Home, but Asian Americans Sometimes Feel Treated as Outlanders with Unproven Loyalties," *Time*, September 25, 2000.

William Claiborne, "Supremacy Group Faces Fateful Trial," *Washington Post,* August 28, 2000.

Lynette Clemetson, "The New Victims of Hate," *Newsweek*, November 6, 2000.

————, "Trying to Right Mr. Wong: The Web Site's Founders Say It's Entertainment. But Asian-Americans Say It's Offensive—and Dangerous," *Newsweek*, July 31, 2000.

"Closet Racism," *Broadcasting and Cable*, September 11, 2000.

Sarah Cohen and D'Vera Cohn, "Racial Integration's Shifting Patterns," *Washington Post*, April 1, 2001.

D'Vera Cohn and Darryl Fears, "Hispanics Draw Even with Blacks in New Census," *Washington Post*, March 7, 2001.

Ilene Cooper, "To Bigotry No Sanction: The Story of the Oldest Synagogue in America" [book review], *Booklist*, February 1, 1999.

Paul Cotton, "Gay, Lesbian Physicians Meet, March, Tell Shalala Bigotry Is Health Hazard," *Journal of the American Medical Association*, May 26, 1993.

Daniela Deane, "Mortgage Study Finds a Rise in Racial Bias," *Washington Post*, September 16, 1999.

John S. DeMott, "The Racism Next Door; Segregated Housing Is Still a Blight in Most Neighborhoods," *Time*, June 30, 1986.

D. Stanley Eitzen and Maxine Baca Zinn, "The Dark Side of Sports Symbols," *USA Today Magazine*, January 2001.

R. E. Blake Evans, "One Nation, but Not Equal," *Builder*, February 2000.

Paul Farhi, "Reality TV Broadcasts 'Bad Black Guy' Stereotype," *Washington Post*, February 20, 2001.

Kevin Fedarko, "Chicago's Last Hope," *Time*, April 7, 1997.

Michael A. Fletcher, "Penn State Students Protest Racist Threats," *Washington Post*, May 2, 2001.

Sherry Godfrey, Charles L. Richman, and Taryn N. Withers, "Reliability and Validity of a New Scale to Measure Prejudice: The GRISMS," *Current Psychology*, Spring 2000.

"Hate Crimes: Should They Receive Special Attention?" *Christian Science Monitor*, June 23, 2000.

Paul Hendrickson, "Mississippi Haunting," *Washington Post* (magazine), February 27, 2000.

Nat Hentoff, "Black Bigotry and Free Speech," *Progressive*, May 1994.

Barbara Holden-Smith, "Lynching, Federalism, and the Intersection of Race and Gender in the Progressive Era," *Yale Journal of Law and Feminism*, 1996.

Dobie Holland, "Is Racism Increasing in America?" *Jet*, April 29, 1996.

"Inside Skinhead," *Utne Reader*, July/August 1998.

Richard D. Kahlenberg, *Race* [book review], *Washington Post*, February 4, 2001.

Tom Kenworthy, "McKinney Avoids Death Sentence," *Washington Post*, November 5, 1999.

Brad Knickerbocker, "New Face of Racism in America," *Christian Science Monitor*, January 14, 2000.

Kenneth Labich, "No More Crude at Texaco," *Fortune*, September 6, 1999.

Wilhelmina A. Leigh, "Institutional Racism, Part III: Racism or Preference? The Role of 'Soft Skills' in Hiring," *Nation's Cities Weekly*, June 26, 2000.

Claude-Anne Lopez, "Prophet and Loss: Benjamin Franklin, the Jews, and Cyber-Bigotry," *New Republic*, January 27, 1997.

Alair MacLean, "Bigotry and Poison," *Progressive*, January 1993.

Jay Mathews, "Study Finds Racial Bias in Special Ed," *Washington Post*, March 3, 2001.

John Maynard, "MTV Blackout to Target Issue of Hate Crimes," *Washington Post*, January 5, 2001.

John P. McAlpin, "Charges Against Trooper Pared," *Washington Post*, October 26, 2000.

"Mind Your Own Mascot," *Newsweek*, November 27, 2000.

David Neiwert, "Hate Group Loses Property to Two Who Won Lawsuit," *Washington Post*, February 14, 2001.

Kimberly Shearer Palmer, "MTV: Battling Hate Online," *Washington Post*, February 1, 2001.

Annie Murphy Paul, "Where Bias Begins: The Truth About Stereotypes," *Psychology Today*, June 1998.

"Race and Recognition," *Washington Post*, December 4, 2000.

"Redefining Race in America: Special Report," *Newsweek*, September 18, 2000.

"Rooting Out Racism," *Business Week*, January 10, 2000.

Megan Rosenfeld, "MTV with a Conscience," *Washington Post*, January 10, 2001.

Dale Russakoff, "Expressions of Pride, Worries of Prejudice," *Washington Post*, August 8, 2000.

Rene Sanchez, "White Supremacist Enters Guilty Plea," *Washington Post*, January 25, 2001.

Sarah Schafer, "Settling Lawsuits with a Gesture," *Washington Post*, February 11, 2001.

David Segal, "Grammys' Discordant Note," *Washington Post*, January 5, 2001.

Vern E. Smith and Andrew Murr, "Up from Jim Crow," *Newsweek*, September 18, 2000.

Charlene Marmer Solomon, "Keeping Hate out of the Workplace," *Personnel Journal*, July 1992.

Thomas Sowell, "Lucrative Bigotry," *Forbes*, May 9, 1994.

Carol Starr, "White Women Working Together on Personal and Institutional Racism," *American Libraries*, March 1988.

Lauren Tarshis, "Brotherhood of Bigots," *Scholastic Update*, April 3, 1992.

————, "The Voice of a Victim," *Scholastic Update*, April 3, 1992.

Stacy A. Teicher, "Schools Atop Dumps: Environmental Racism?" *Christian Science Monitor*, November 4, 1999.

Evan Thomas, Bob Cohn, and Howard Fineman, "Rethinking the Dream," *Newsweek*, June 26, 1995.

Chris Tilly, "Institutional Racism, Part II: Race, Skill, and Hiring in U.S. Cities," *Nation's Cities Weekly*, June 19, 2000.

Patrick Welsh, "At T. C. Williams, Separate Fields of Play," *Washington Post*, October 22, 2000.

Jack E. White, "Imus 'n' Andy: The Radio Host and His Sidekicks Trade in Bigotry," *Time*, May 22, 2000.

Heather Wisner, "Grace Under Fire," *Dance Magazine*, February 2001.

James Zogby, "The Politics of Exclusion," *Civil Rights Journal*, Fall 1998.

Internet Sources

American Civil Liberties Union, "'Consumer Racism' Suit Ends in Million Dollar Judgment," October 13, 1997. www.aclu.org/news/101397c.html.

Anti-Defamation League, "Close the Book on Hate." www.adl.org/ctboh/kids_do.html.

————, "Counteracting Hate Crimes: A National Priority," October 1997. www.adl.org/opinion/counter_hatecrimes.html.

————, "Explosion of Hate: The Growing Danger of the National Alliance," 2000. www.adl.org/explosion_of_hate/ explosion_of_hate.html.

————, "Hate Crimes Laws," 1999. www.adl.org/99hatecrime.

————, "The International Jew: Anti-Semitism from the Roaring Twenties Revived on the Web," July 1999. www.adl.org/special_reports/ij/intro.html.

————, "Poisoning the Web: Holocaust Denial," 2000. www.adl.org/poisoning_web/holocaust_denial.html.

————, "Resistance Records a Cash Cow for Hate Movement" [press release], June 5, 2000. www.adl.org/PresRele/Asus_12/3620_12.html.

————, "Responding to Extremist Speech Online: 10 Frequently Asked Questions." www.adl.org/issue_combating_hate/10faq.

Associated Press, "A Hate-Filled Heart," *CNNSI.com*, January 7, 2000. www.sportsillustrated.cnn.com/baseball/mlb/news/2000/01/07/rocker_reax_ap/index.html.

Don Bowman, "Remembering the Titans: In 1971, an Integrated High School Football Team Won More than the Virginia State Title; It Also Beat Racism," *Knight-Ridder/Tribune News Service*, October 19, 2000. www.star-telegram.com.

Raju Chebium, "Attorney Morris Dees Pioneer in Using 'Damage Litigation' to Fight Hate Groups," *CNN.com*, September 8, 2000. www.cnn.com/2000/LAW/09/08/morris.dees.profile/index.html.

"Coke Settles Discrimination Suit," *About.com*, December 2000. racerelations.about.com/newsissues/racerelations/library/weekly/aa112000a.htm.

"Coke to Settle Race Bias Case for $192.5 Million," *Muzi.com News*, November 17, 2000. www.dailynews.muzi.com.

Dave Cullen, "The Reluctant Activist," *Salon News*, October 15, 1999. www.salon.com/news/feature/1999/10/15/laramie.

"Cuomo Says Million Dollar Award Sends Clear Message Against Racial Discrimination on the Internet," HUD Press Release No. 00-165, July 20, 2000. www.hud.gov/pressrel/pr00-165.html.

George E. Curry, "Racism Costs Corporate America," *New Journal & Guide*, December 7, 2000. www.njournalg.com/editorial/2000/12/curr_racism_costs.html.

Katie Dean, "MS on Racism: We Did Our Best," *Wired*, July 1, 1999. www.wired.com/news/politics/0,1283,20536,00.html.

Morris Dees and Ellen Bowden, "Taking Hate Groups to Court," February 1995. www.splcenter.org.

Bryan Denson, "Mulugeta Seraw's Death a Decade Ago Avenged," *Oregonian*, November 13, 1998. www.oregonlive.com/cgi-bin/printer/printer.cgi.

John Derbyshire, "In Defense of Racial Profiling," *National Review*, February 19, 2001. www.nationalreview.com/19feb01/derbyshire021901.shtml.

Lyndon Baines Johnson, "Special Message to the Congress: The American Promise," Lyndon Baines Johnson Library and Museum home page, March 15, 1965. www.lbjlib.utexas.edu/johnson/archives.hom/speeches.hom/special_messages.asp.

"Jury Finds Against Aryan Nations for $6.3 Million," *CNN.com*, September 7, 2000. www.cnn.com/2000/LAW/09/07/aryan.verdict.

Kirin Kalia, "Politically Internet: Icebox's Controversial Mr. Wong Takes Heat," *Digital Coast Daily*, September 15, 2000. www.digitalcoastdaily.com/issues/dcw09152000.html.

Sheila Kaplan, "The New Face of Racism," *U.S. News & World Report*, January 3, 2000. www.usnews.com/usnews/issue/000103/race.htm.

Matt Katz, "Racism in Three Pieces Is Still Racism," *Daily Illini*, April 17, 1997. www.daily.illini.com/archives/1997/April/17/p13_katzcol.txt.html.

Donna Ladd, "Living in Terror," *Village Voice*, May 17, 2000. www.villagevoice.com/issues/0020/ladd.shtml.

Doris Lin, "The Death of (Icebox.com's) Mr. Wong," *USAsians.net*, 2001. www.geocities.com/Hollywood/Palace/2713/articles-mrwong.html.

John P. McAlpin, "Lawyer: Cops Still Look at Race," Associated Press, April 3, 2001. www.washingtonpost.com/wp-srv/aponline/20010403/aponline2345846_000.htm.

Dennis McCafferty, "Desperately Seeking Angry White Females," *Salon News*, October 14, 1999. www.salon.com/news/feature/1999/10/14/hate/index.html.

"McKinney Guilty of Murder," *ABCNEWS.com*, November 3, 1999. abcnews.go.com/sections/us/DailyNews/Shepard_verdict.html.

"Men Avoid Prison with Guilty Pleas in Chicago Racial Beating," *CNN.com*, October 19, 1998. www.cnn.com/US/9810/19/racial.beating.

Jeannine Mjoseth, "Psychologists Call for Assault on Hate Crimes," *APA Monitor*, January 1998. www.apa.org/monitor/jan98/hate.html.

John Frederick Moore, "Suit Alleges MSFT Racism," *CNNfn.com*, June 30, 1999. www.cnnfn.com/output/pfv/1999/06/30/technology/microsoft.

Kim Murphy, "Government Seeks to Stop Internet 'Stalking,'" *Bergen Record*, February 13, 2000. www.bergen.com/morenews/cybersta200002131.htm.

———, "Lawsuits Threaten to Drain the Life out of Hate Groups," *Los Angeles Times*, August 22, 2000. www.latimes.com.

National Alliance, "What Is the National Alliance? National Alliance Goals." www.natvan.com.

———, "Who Rules America?" June 2000. www.natvan.com/who-rules-america.

Jeff Pearlman, "At Full Blast," *Sports Illustrated Online*, December 23, 1999. sportsillustrated.cnn.com/features/cover/news/1999/12/22/rocker.

David Pilgrim, "The Brute Caricature," Jim Crow Museum of Racist Memorabilia, November 2000. www.ferris.edu/news/jimcrow.

Public Broadcasting System, "Clinton Sipes' Story," *Not in Our Town.* www.pbs.org/niot/programs/clinton.htm.

Faye Rice, "Denny's Changes Its Spots," *Fortune*, May 12, 1996. www. fortune.com/fortune/magazine/1996/960513/managing3. html.

Mike Robinson, "Chicago Trial Puts Focus on Racial Tensions," Associated Press, April 18, 1998. www.nando.net/newsroom/ntn/nation/041898/nationt_9380_body.html.

Gregory D. Squires, "The Indelible Color Line," *American Prospect,* January 1999. www.prospect.org/authors/squires-g.html.

DeWayne Wickham, "They Suffer for Doing Right Thing," *USA Today*, May 16, 2000. www.usatoday.com/news/comment/columnists/wickham/wick093.htm.

James Willwerth, "Confessions of a Skinhead," *Time*, August 19, 1996. www.time.com/time/magazine/archive/1996/dom/960819/skins.html.

World Church of the Creator, "Frequently Asked Questions About Creativity." www.creator.org/faq.html.

Websites

HateWatch (www.hatewatch.org). HateWatch is a Web-based organization that monitors the activities of hate groups on the Internet.

Jim Crow Museum of Racist Memorabilia (www.ferris. edu/news/jimcrow). Sociology professor David Pilgrim has collected materials documenting the history of racism against African Americans. The on-line collection includes in-depth analyses as well as pictures of many of the items in the museum, which is located in Big Rapids, Michigan.

National Criminal Justice Reference Service (www.ncjrs.org). This organization collects and publishes data on crime in the United States, including information on hate crimes.

Public Broadcasting System: Not in Our Town
(www.pbs.org/niot/programs/niot1.htm). This site is related to
the PBS documentary on how Billings, Montana, responded to
a surge of hate violence in 1993. Besides telling the story, the
site includes information on related incidents and antihate programs across the country.

Index

Picture Credits

Cover photo: © Richard B. Levine
© AFP/CORBIS, 9, 18, 78, 90
AP Photo/Tom Davenport, 57
AP Photo/Kevork Djansezian, 38
AP Photo/File, 92
AP Photo/Mark Foley, 47
AP Photo/Michael S. Green, 64
AP Photo/Clark Jones, 39
AP Photo/David Karp, 85
AP Photo/Wilfredo Lee, 88
AP Photo/Dan Loh, 66
AP Photo/Rene Macura, 62
AP Photo/Bebeto Matthews, 81
AP Photo/Michael Okoniewski, 42
AP Photo/Kari Shuda, 60
AP Photo/Tribune Review/Marc Fader, 83
Archive Photos, 26
© Bettmann/CORBIS, 22, 23, 32
© CORBIS, 49
Library of Congress, 21, 76
©Adam Mastoon/CORBIS, 33
National Archives, 15, 27
North Wind Picture Archives, 19
© Tim O'Hara/CORBIS, 53
PhotoDisc, 51
Reuters/Jeff T. Green/Archive Photos, 74
© Reuters NewMedia Inc./CORBIS, 10, 28, 67, 72
© Joseph Sohm; ChromoSohm Inc./CORBIS, 95
© David & Peter Turnley/CORBIS, 35, 36, 45
© Underwood & Underwood/CORBIS, 59

About the Author

Debbie Levy writes non-fiction, fiction, and poetry for adults and children. Her work on topics ranging from law to parenting to cyberspace has appeared in books, as well as in such publications as the *Washington Post, Legal Times, Washington Parent,* and *Highlights for Children.* Before turning to her writing career, Ms. Levy practiced law with a large Washington, D.C. law firm, and served as an editor for a national chain of newspapers for lawyers. She earned a B.A. in government and foreign affairs from the University of Michigan. Ms. Levy enjoys kayaking and fishing in the Chesapeake Bay region, hiking just about anywhere, and playing the piano. She lives with her husband and their two sons in Chevy Chase, Maryland.